SHADOW

Printed in Australia
First Printing: April 2023

Paperback ISBN 978-1-7637569-3-9
Hardcover ISBN 978-1-7637569-5-3
Ebook ISBN 978-1-7637569-4-6

Cyber Unicorns
www.cyberunicorns.com.au

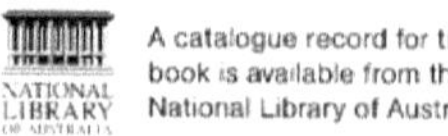
A catalogue record for this book is available from the National Library of Australia

SHADOW

CRAIG FORD

THE RENDEZVOUS

I am making my way into Brisbane city. Sam and her team are about to conduct a surveillance op in Brisbane city, someone selling some stolen data or something, that doesn't matter to me though. I just care about the fact that she is going to be out in the open and I need to figure out how I can arrange a conversation with her. I head in with a couple cars, just in case I need to switch rides a few times on my exit. I will send in one of the other cars to scoop up Sam and lose any tails if needed before I join her. I can easily watch from one of the other cars and keep at a safe distance.

I watch the exchange take place and the teams break off. The main group follows the foreign agent and Sam wanders down the street, casually keeping an eye on her target. I have a feeling that agent is going to have a really bad day. I don't think it will be long before they drag him in for interrogation. This is my chance to get her alone.

'Sarina, take the tesla and stop her midway across the pedestrian crossing she is heading towards. Once she is stopped, wait for her to get in.'

I watch Sarina come to an aggressive stop right in front of Sam. It would appear she is startled by the sudden appearance of the car and takes a few steps back. I get out my phone and type a message to Sam: *Get in*. Simple. Straight to the point.

Sam takes her phone out of her pocket while others walk around the car blocking the crossing. She just keeps looking at the message. I guess deciding if she wants to go down this path or not. I don't have time for this. I repeat my message: *Get in, Sam.*

She steps forward after a few seconds, seemingly deciding to go with it. She grabs the handle and slides into the back seat.

'Sarina, take her a few suburbs away and set up a rendezvous point so I can get in the car with her.' As Sam's door closes, the car surges to life. I wonder what Sam thinks of the no driver, it can be quite terrifying the first time. I still sometimes have the urge to take over, but honestly, Sarina is probably a better driver than I am.

Almost twenty minutes go by and I get out of my car just before the intersection. I'll get in the car at the traffic lights. Sarina will make sure the lights are red long enough to allow me to enter the car. I make my way over and I can see several cars approaching the intersection, including Sam in the Tesla. The lights turn red and the cars stop. My turn to make an entrance. I step out onto the street walking directly towards the car. I take a deep breath. Here we go. I grab the handle and slide in the car next to Sam.

As I enter the car and close the door, I can see Sam looks unsure about the situation. She glances at the door, her fingers reaching for the door handle. She furrows her eyebrows a little. I know this kind of situation is probably not one she feels comfortable in, especially after what she has gone through recently with the cartel. Random people just jumping into the car at an intersection would not be making her feel very safe at all. I'm impressed though, as she takes a deep breath and calms herself. As soon as the car door closes, the car surges forward. Sarina is getting some distance from anyone who could be trying to follow us.

'Sarina, change tesla one's colour to grey. Avoid surveillance zones.' I see Sam look at me with a judgemental quirk of her eyebrow, as if she's wondering, *what drugs is this guy on? A car can't just change colour or drive by itself.* I study her as Sarina initiates the change on the cars nanoshell. Sam looks in awe of what is happening, her eyes are wide with fascination. If she doesn't arrest me, I'm certain I'll be spending some time explaining about the car and Sarina, but for now, I have pressing matters we need to discuss.

'I missed you Sam. You look good.' She holds my gaze. I know, I know, pressing matters and all I want to do is say I missed her? Get a hold of yourself Shadow.

A few more moments go by and she folds her arms over her chest. 'So, what is this all about? What do you want?' I'm a little thrown by her directness and my stomach twists into knots.

I take a deep breath. 'I need your help...' I take another breath. 'I've gotten myself into a bit of a situation. I was trying to distract myself and went after a criminal hacking group called Arachnid. I think I may have bitten off more than I can chew.'

Her eyebrow quirks, 'What did you do? What sort of trouble are you in?'

Where do I start... maybe I need to go back to the beginning.

6 MONTHS EARLIER...

CHAPTER 1

MY IDENTITY

I've lived in this identity for almost a year now. I'm truly starting to sink into this role, this new me. I think I'm enjoying being Jacob Loxley. He is my fifth identity since I started this mission. I've been burned a few times when I was careless or I bailed when someone was getting a little too close. I couldn't have anyone get to know me too well. I keep people at a distance and move on if it starts to become an issue.

Once I abandon an identity, it is cleaned. Nothing of mine is left behind, no photos, nothing. Like it never existed. I would wipe people's memories if I could, but it is not necessary. For most, I was just a blip they don't remember. Nothing or no one of consequence. It is strange though, isn't it? That someone could live a shadow of a life, one that doesn't exist, doesn't connect with anyone around them. Just exist, so to speak.

I have done this many times and I'm getting good at it. I interact enough for everyone to believe the lie. I go to parties, I talk to girls, but not enough to make anyone want more from me. Just enough so people will know who I am if asked but they won't remember much more.

Jacob is a university student at the Brisbane technical college, one of the most renowned universities in the country, for only the brightest minds, at least that's what the brochure says. I think it is just a bunch of teenagers, getting drunk, taking drugs and plotting their massive game or app that is supposedly going to make them all rich. Every second day one of them is having a party. It never stops. Just party, party and more parting. I don't know how some of them are passing their classes. I guess some of them really are that smart, maybe the brochure is right. I join them in the festivities on occasion, but generally I keep to myself.

Tonight, I'm in one of those moods where I want to push back on the pain and drown some of my sorrows. A self-pity party. Alcohol and drugs I'm sure are the worst way to do it but tonight I drink with my housemates. They are certainly different but they do know how to have a good time. They are always the life of any party.

Across the room is a girl who has been watching me most of the night. She smiles whenever I see her looking. She is pretty and is not trying to hide that she has been watching me. I want to have some fun, meet a nice girl, but if I do, she might get too close and I might have to abandon this life. I'm enjoying being Jacob. The name suits me and I have been able to stay in this life longer than any other. I don't want to screw it up now.

I've been holding her gaze for too long. She takes that as an indication for her to make a move, and approaches me, coming in nice and close to talk.

'I'm Sarah, you're Jacob, right?'

I look at her for a few moments, mildly concerned my identity has preceded our interaction. Have I gotten sloppy? 'Yes, that's right.'

She smiles at me and moves a little closer. She really is very pretty. This close, I can see the faintest shimmer from a speck of silver eyeshadow that has fallen from her eyelid. I feel she would not be happy with such an imperfection. Every other detail, her hair, her makeup, is perfect. Exactly how it should be, just that one speck. One minor imperfection.

'Jacob, I've been watching you. There is something mysterious about you. Almost a bad boy vibe. Are you a bad boy?'

She's laying this on thick and I can smell alcohol on her breath. I need to stop this before it goes too far. I open my mouth, ready to say I'm going to head home and it was nice to meet her, when she leans into me and plants a kiss on my mouth. She tastes like strawberry. I assume it's some sort of lip gloss or something. Her lips are firm and passionate. I almost for a second forget everything around me. I forget who I am. I'm enjoying being with Sarah; who she thinks I am doesn't feel important right now. A few heated moments pass and she starts to move her hands over my body. I'm at a turning point. I either go with this and down that rabbit hole or I stop it now. I need to make a choice and fast.

I lean back and pull our lips apart. She looks me in the eyes, trying to figure out what is happening. By the looks of her reaction, people don't say no to her. I get it, she is very pretty and could easily wrap most guys around her finger, but I'm not most guys. Her fake blonde bimbo act is not for me. Yeah, I'm alive and I still have a pulse, I can't deny she is friggin' gorgeous but I don't want that. I want something more than just good looks. I want to find someone who can challenge me, who can be my true equal, maybe even my better. This girl is not her, of that, I'm sure.

I need to do something before she makes another move.

'Look, Sarah, I think you are a good looking girl but I'm seeing someone at the moment.' I'm not, but it seems the kindest way to let her down. She tilts her head and looks at me for a few moments, it looks like she is deciding if that matters to her. Looks like it does.

'Sorry. I didn't know.'

'Thanks, don't worry about it. I better go. Have a good night, okay?'

She nods and heads back over to her friends, who are all giggling at what just happened. I grab my coat and head for the door.

As I leave, I see the boys over with some girls and just give them a quick wave. They give me a nod. They don't argue, it's pretty normal for me to just leave when I'm over the party. They seem to ride out the whole night but don't seem to mind if I bail on shenanigans. I find the door with a quick review of the room and make my way out.

That's enough of an adventure for me tonight. Enough of the real world.

CHAPTER 2

IN THE BEGINNING

I am way too buzzed to go to sleep after what just happened at the party. I have been scoping out a new target lately and might as well just do a quick check in to see what he is up too. No point heading home just yet, I might as well get to work.

I am sitting in the dark, my car parked a few blocks away from home, watching my latest target from my laptop screen. He is a family man. I know this because he's playing with his kids in their room, they are laughing and having a great time. They are up a little late but he isn't making a big deal out of it, just enjoying their company. I can tune in via his CCTV feed—which he left open to the internet with default credentials in it. Sometimes the challenge isn't even worth getting out of bed for.

I'm a hacker. I'm feared in the underbelly of our digital world. I'm the definition of the bogeyman for anyone lurking in these deeply hidden regions of cyberspace, reaching far beyond the digital space right into the real lives of anyone who dares interfere. I give no remorse or sympathy to my victims; they are collateral in a war. Nothing more.

I wasn't always like this. I was a gentle, loving boy, with parents that adored me. I remember my childhood very clearly, they were the happy times of my life, a time when life seemed much simpler. I would spend hours playing at the park or with my favourite toy. It's hard to fight back a smile when I remember back on those days.

I wanted for nothing, I had everything I could ever need or want. My father, Peter, was from a wealthy family and was CEO of a big company involved in natural resources. You know, mining, gas, that sort of thing. He worked hard, but family always came first. My mum, Monique, and he were in love. It was so strong, it was almost infectious.

My mother was very beautiful. I still remember her vividly from those days, a truly rare beauty. I could see why my father would have first noticed her, but it was a beauty that ran deep. It radiated from her, like some kind of aura, a beauty both on the surface and within. She was an amazing woman who honestly could influence my father like no other could. He was a powerful man and was used to getting what he wanted, he would wave a hand and people would just do as he asked but not with my mother. It was different between them.

They had mutual respect, neither had a stronger influence over the other. They were a true team. One full of love. I was an only child and they shared a similar level of love for me as they did for one another. I could always feel their love.

We would go on trips around the world every few weeks. China, Japan, USA, Europe, New Zealand, Indonesia and so many more places. Dad had to work, that's why we travelled, but he always spent half the time with us and the other half working. He always made sure we were looked after and would take time off at some point to go with us to see the amazing sights, wherever we were. It was an unspoken promise, something we just knew would happen each time.

Dad would do what he needed to do and we would enjoy the resorts and pools. When he was done we would all go together. I know my childhood was great; I had it so much better than so many people. I should value those memories, use them to make my life better. I should find a love like my parents had, an all-consuming love, one that means more than anything else.

I don't know how to do that though, my heart is poisoned, black with little love in it anymore. I'm driven by a need to crush my enemies, to make them all pay. Nothing else matters to me. It's almost intoxicating and I know deep down this path is not the best for me but I can't shake it off. I know what I am. I embrace it. I'm Shadow, the hacker that punishes those who go too far, those who take what is not theirs and have no thought for their victims. What happened to my once perfect family made me this way, made me who I am. Or at least set me on this path.

As Shadow, a dark, tormented hacker, I feel powerful and purpose-driven. I feel at home, with my life. Lately, I'm getting a little darker and more aggressive with my enemies. I'm showing no sympathy or emotion, it's just another job. I'm losing myself more and more to this world and I'm not sure if I should fight it or embrace it even further.

The feeling I get when I'm on the hunt is like a drug. My mind seems to unlock parts of myself I didn't know existed and I can bend any systems to my will. I can find anyone, crush their world in a matter of hours. Nothing can stop me.

I have come up against a lot of other hackers, some good, some lame, but none of them have presented a real challenge for me. I was like a teacher herding children running around a schoolyard. They didn't even slow me down. I would enjoy the challenge of going up against someone of real skill but there is not many of us out there, true elites, the ones who are only whispered about because of the fear they inspire. The true artists. I know someone has to be able to match my skills, or maybe even better them. I hope I get to meet them someday. I think it could be fun to truly be challenged.

I guess none of that family stuff matters anymore. Life isn't what it used to be. I don't see myself having what they had. This is my hand and I'll go with it. I'll embrace my lot and truly be Shadow. It's funny, Shadow started as my cover, my name to hide my true self, but it turns out Shadow may be my true self and Mark Matthews is my fake self. That's my "real name" if there is such a thing—my family name. That's the real value I place on it, my father's name. It still means something to me, even if not much else in this world does.

I refocus, trying to pay attention to the task at hand. I crack my knuckles and stare at the screen in front of me. Watching this guy playing with his kids makes me hope he is remorseful, to want to change. I don't want to ruin those kids lives because their father values money and power over them. I don't want to set them on the same path as me.

I sigh. This is going to be his lucky day. I am going to give him a warning shot, for his kids. He deserves the chance to prove he is a good dad, to give his kids the opportunity to have a great life, to have a great dad like I did.

He won't get a second chance though.

I load up my phone emulator and start to type a message.

'I am Shadow. I am watching you. I know what you have done. Those two kids you are playing with are the only reason I haven't ruined your life, taken back what you have stolen and made you regret ever crossing paths with me. You have one chance. Only one. Set right what you have done, be a better father, or next time you will not see me coming.'

I hit send. Maybe a little melodramatic but it will get my message across. I wait a few moments for the message to flash on his phone. As I watch, he picks his phone up and reads my message. Eyes wide, he looks around, confused. Then he slowly lifts his eyes to the camera nestled in the corner of the room, realisation setting in. He looks at his kids for a few moments and then back at the camera and nods.

I truly hope this is not just a show and he changes course for his kids' sake. I guess time will tell.

CHAPTER 3

MY DAD

I wonder if he will truly do the right thing. Will their lives change at this moment for the better? Will he choose them, or will their lives go down the same path mine did? Will he continue down a path of destruction, one of no return? This man and his kids make me think about how my own life could have been different, if things hadn't changed.

My life started to change when I was around thirteen or so. My father was working a bit more than usual. He told us he was working on something big that would allow us to spend more time together. I thought he must have been stepping down as CEO and letting one of his seconds take the reins. We would still own the company and earn a lot of money from it, so it made sense he could step aside and allow others to do the day-to-day things.

I was wrong. It turned out my father had been scammed by some thug on the stock exchange. Some sort of investment firm guy had convinced my father to leverage everything we had to invest in this perfect stock he said was going to go through the roof. My father borrowed against the house, the business, everything we had, but it didn't go the way it was supposed to. It fell through the floor. The stock lost all of its perceived value, hundreds of millions overnight. Everyone, not just my family, but everyone else that was convinced to put money into this scheme, lost all their money.

Somehow, the con artist of a trader didn't lose any money. He still got all his commissions on the sales and in turn, lost the life savings of so many people. When the victims questioned what happened all he said was, 'That's the stock market for you.'

After a few months, we lost our house, the business and everything we had. Everything was gone. We could barely afford to pay rent on a nasty apartment near the city.

I think the hardest part for my dad was the company. His father had left it to him, his grandfather had left it to his father before that; several generations past had built a legacy for us. He had lost it to a crook.

Dad tried to pick himself up—he got a day job working in the city. He was a smart guy and people could use his skills, but it was never the same. He started to drink a lot, come home less often, and I could see my parents growing slowly apart. The love I had seen as a child was fading away. My mother tried to help him see how much he still had, but he couldn't see it. He couldn't shake off the demons in his mind; all he saw was failure.

It went on like this for a few years, until one day I came home to the sound of my mother sobbing. When I found her, I saw something I would never be able to unsee.

He had shot himself. A pistol in the mouth and brains splattered all over the wall behind his desk.

I was almost sixteen the last time I saw my father; the day he took his life. I wish I could have told him how much he meant to me, showed him we were there for him. We didn't resent the new life. It wasn't his fault.

My mother lost her spark that day, and if I'm honest, I don't think I've ever been the same either. How could anyone be after seeing that?

She took her life a few months later.

I guess it all just got too much for her. Nothing as explosive as my father. She took too many sleeping pills and didn't wake up. I buried both my parents before I was seventeen.

I had the best parents in the world and I lost them to their inner demons. All because of a crook who cared more about money and power than he did about any of those families he crushed. Not just my own, hundreds of families with life savings thrown down the drain at his whim. He gets richer and everyone else gets poorer. How can this be what is acceptable in our society, how can someone like him get away with doing this to people over and over for their gain? He was a con artist and needed to be stopped.

I tried to find a legal way to get him to pay for what he did. I had no money though and no lawyer would take on the case. They all said it was a lost cause, he had too much money and could fight us in court for years until my money ran out. I would never beat him that way.

I told the police what happened and gave them all the evidence that he was just conning people but they didn't care. There wasn't anything illegal about what he was doing. They agreed it was pretty horrible but still, nothing illegal. He operated within the confines of the law so there was nothing anyone would do to help make him pay. There must be something, someone, who could help me.

I never did find anyone who would or could help.

CHAPTER 4

TAKING BACK WHAT WAS MINE

The birth of Shadow, my hacker self, came out of necessity. I had tried to get justice for what had happened to my family, but no one would help me. This man was too rich and powerful for anyone to go after him. People were either scared of the consequences or just said it would be too costly. I don't blame them. A lot of them had families, businesses to look out for, and this was not a fight they thought they could win. I get it, but that didn't help me.

I had always been a bit of a natural with computers and anything electronic really for as long as I can remember. My mother was the same. She'd had a secret skill she never told my father. She was a hacker. Quite a good one, if you ask me. She never did anything outrageous or illegal from what I know, but who knows what she could have got up to in secret.

What I do know is that she was a type of activist. She would help bring attention to important causes, help pull down sites that represented bad people. She had been teaching and helping hone my skills from when I was around ten. She said I needed to learn how to do it right and it was going to be something special, just between us. Just a mother and son thing. It remained that way and we never discussed any of that with anyone other than each other.

I think those lessons are what made me such a good hacker. Yes, the natural skills help and I'm sure my mother's abilities passed down to me but I also inherited my father's analytical mind. My mother thought the combination would make me very skilful. I could consider my moves several moves in advance and anticipate my opponents. I was able to beat my mother and her connections in the hidden world on many occasions, before I was even twelve. I don't know if it was my hacker's ability or my analytical mind that enabled me to triumph but I was growing stronger every day.

When I had exhausted all my options for getting justice, I knew what I had to do. Shadow was born. I spent the last of my family's money to buy the systems I needed. I wanted to do this right. I didn't want to do this and get caught, I had to ensure the preparations were in place. I needed to have a fall identity in case things went south and I needed to have a plan. I had to do this right for my parents. This man needed to pay for the pain he caused and I was going to take what was mine, what belonged to my family and what he took from everyone else too. He would have nothing left. I would take what he valued most: Money.

All of it.

I got to work, anonymising my systems, routing all my data and activity through multiple locations and then rerouting them. I created what was my first fake identity: Michael Johns. It's not a truly relevant name; I used it only once for this job. It was just a way to get accounts and have something to lose the police with false info so they wouldn't look for me, the real me. I had electricity bills, phone bills, credit cards and bank accounts. On paper, this guy existed. It took me a few long days to ensure it was a solid ID.

Reconnaissance was easy. This guy liked to show off his money, flashy cars, parties, social media. Honestly, I'm surprised he hadn't been a target of a hacker before. The sheer arrogance and flashy bull crap he plastered everywhere would be like a red flag to a bull.

I gathered everything I could, learned about his friends, who he hung out with, where and when. I knew everything about this guy. The more I dug, the more I could see my family were not his only victims. Many people commented on his lavish posts about him stealing their money and then living up big on it. The comments were always quickly removed, but I could still see them. Nothing on the internet is ever really gone. He was the bastard I thought he was. He deserved to have done to him what he had done to others.

My plan was starting to come together. If I wanted to stop him doing this in the future, I needed to ensure he couldn't trade anymore. I had to ruin his reputation and then take all of his money. I knew that would mean all of his fake friends too. They were there for the parties, the money. Without that, he was just an arsehole who would be alone to contemplate why this all happened to him.

I wormed my way into all his accounts, took control of all his finances, his home security systems. Like a virus, I spread through everything, hiding, waiting for my moment to strike to repay the debt I was owed.

I don't remember what day it was or even why I chose that particular day. I think it was just when everything was in place and my plan could run its course.

I started by locking him out of all his social media, pushing out all of the filthy horrible content he had collected of himself taking advantage of innocent women, records of his financial schemes and how he stole so many people's money. I put it all out there for all to see. I sent it all to media outlets that started to run with the story. He tried to do damage control, but he was locked out and it was already too late. I sent the same records to the governing body that looks after licences for financial brokers and traders, who were quite swift in suspending his licence. He was being cut off from all angles.

All those friends disappeared as soon as the story broke. No one wanted to be connected to him. He was on his own now, isolated. He was starting to feel some of what my father had but it wasn't over yet.

I filtered all his money out into offshore accounts I had set up in his name. I wanted it to look like he was trying to hide the money, filter it out so the authorities couldn't get their hands on it. I wanted him to look guilty. As soon as I had emptied all his accounts, I initiated repossessions of all his cars, his houses, I took it all. I bounced the money all around so it couldn't be traced, then I moved my family's money into an account. It wasn't all of it, but what I thought was fair. The rest, I set up an automated payment of equal amounts into the accounts of everyone he had ruined; the true owners of that hard-earned money. They would get some of their dignity back.

When it was all over, he was arrested and he is still in jail for fraud, rape and several other charges. I don't see him getting out anytime soon. Justice was served. A bad man was made to pay for his crimes and what was stolen was returned to those who truly owned it.

I'd trashed the identity I had made for the job and erased my presence. I had never existed and I had never touched any of the accounts. I was just a shadow, a thought no one could pin down. I'm sure both the scumbag sitting in jail and the police, still don't know what really happened. Maybe even still scratch their heads when they think about it. Justice is done and that's all that matters. My mother would be proud of me for what I did. My dad, I don't know, but I feel at ease with my decisions.

I did the right thing.

CHAPTER 5

CONTINUED MISSION

I shut down my laptop and stretch the stiffness from my neck. The night is dark outside the confines of my car. I should head for home, although there's not much waiting for me there. My housemates will still be out for a few more hours. Tonight has reminded me of how I started down this road, but now I'm so far down it, I don't think there's any way back.

I start the car and pull out into the road, heading down the deserted streets to home.

After the job with the con man, I'd lain low for about a year. I didn't want to draw attention to myself. I did small, quiet jobs and some travelling, nothing too flashy, just visiting some of the places I had when I was a child with my parents. Sort of reminiscing, really, thinking about better times. I'm struggling though if I'm honest, I've gotten revenge for my parents. I have most of my family wealth back and I should be happy but I'm not.

I'd still felt the darkness in my heart. A hollowness just keeps eating at me, even now. I guess it's true what people say, 'Money or revenge won't make you happy.' It's true. I've gotten both but if it's possible, I think I feel worse. I didn't have a mission anymore, a reason to push on, to fight. My mind had nothing to occupy itself. I needed to find a new purpose in life, something that could be fulfilling.

I thought about it for a while and toyed with the idea of doing what I did for my family for other families. I had the skills and the willingness to stand up for the people everyone else has either forgotten or just ignores. Why shouldn't I fill my void with something worthwhile?

I planned to find the scum of this earth, the ones who take what isn't theirs, the ones who trample on others to get to the top. Punish them all, take what they have taken from others and give it back. Be like a modern-day Robin Hood. You know, the whole 'take from the rich and give to the poor' thing. Look, I know I'm no saint and I'll keep some of the money for myself to help me do what I do, to hide in plain sight. To vanish when required and keep fighting the good fight.

Everyone has expenses and I thought it will work out good for everyone, except maybe the bad guys I hunt. They would probably get the raw end of the deal and come out a little worse for wear. I thought I should give them a choice: live without all their stolen money, walk away from their dishonest lives and I'll let them be, or I can make them regret ever learning the name Shadow.

It's always felt a little poetic to let them choose. I know most will not go with option number one but when their worlds completely fall apart around them, they know it was their choice. They could have done it a better way, an easier way. One with a little less kerosene on the fire, so to speak. It can be a peaceful transition. I'll let them keep enough money to have a comfortable life, but most of it will need to go back to the people who need it most.

Shadow is a force to be reckoned with, one that deals a blow to anyone who takes advantage of the innocent. It sounds a little corny, I know, but I think it is good use of my gifts and fulfilling for me. Something to ease the pain, make me feel better by doing something for those less fortunate. Be a dark hero of sorts. Okay, maybe hero might be a stretch, but you get it.

I'd gotten to work right away, making several plausible identities to use as cover. I made sure these are even better than the first. These need to hold up for the day-to-day life. People need to believe they are real. Mark Matthews disappeared forever. There was no one left to remember him anyway.

I used my family's recovered money to set up secret bunkers all around the country, secret bases for me to work from. My fake identities cannot touch anything to do with these, none of them can be connected to any of the other identities. Each one is completely separate and is owned by fake corporations. It'd taken months to get everything ready. I used multiple contractors to do different parts of the jobs, isolated from each other so no one knows who or what it is exactly they are building. I think they'd all thought it was some conspiracy theory nuts survival bunker and I guess it kind of ended up that way, just not from a bomb or invasion. They are secret high-tech hacker bases, to help annihilate my targets and keep what I'm doing safe from spying eyes.

I think of them now kinda like my bat cave. I have enough digital firepower to take out an entire army in each of them. I just need a good butler now and I'll be set. That's not going to happen anytime soon though. These bunkers are masterpieces in themselves, multiple redundancies for power, communications, and I could live in any of them for months if I had to. They are like a resort underground, just with no butler. There I go with the butler idea again, no matter how much I want one it's not going to happen.

I arrive back at the house and just as I'd expected, it's deserted. There's no sign of the boys, aside from scattered beer bottles around the lounge from their pre-drinks. I sigh and head for my room. It's easier this way, but I can't deny it's lonely sometimes.

CHAPTER 6

NEXT TARGET

I wake to my alarm clock. It's 6 am. I'm a little tired and foggy from last night. The memory of my interaction at the party with Sarah comes flooding back. I know I did the right thing but sometimes it would be nice to be a normal guy with a normal life—a life that included a girlfriend. That's not my life though. This whole university existence is my fake identity, not my real world.

Could it be different though? Could I stop my hidden life and be Jacob? Would it be possible? Could I find a nice girl and form a real relationship, like a normal person? I laugh a little to myself at that thought, yeah, right, that is so not me.

I get up and jump in the shower. I need to get on the road before the neighbourhood starts to come alive. It is a quick shower; I'm keen to get moving. Throwing on some clothes, I grab my bag and head out the door. My phone gets left on the side table; I don't want to take anything that could allow anyone to track me. In the car, I drive off down the street. It's time to head out west. Time to do my next job.

I take the long way around, always ensuring no one is following me. I can't make a mistake. If I'm followed, I'll need to burn this life and get out of Brisbane. It's nice here. The weather is warm, people are nice. Maybe a little too nice sometimes. Sarah jumps back into my mind again for a few moments. Okay, maybe I do regret that move last night but there's no going back.

I'm getting close to the bunker now. I backtrack a little and circle around the area before I decide to go in. I pull up to the gate, I place my thumb on the scanner at the gate.

'Please provide voiceprint verification,' sounds from the panel speaker.

I take a quick breath, 'Darkness hunts what light can't reach. The truth will shine bright on shadows of the deep and send the unworthy back to the depths to be forgotten.' After a few moments, the indicator on the panel turns green and the gate starts to open.

I drive forward slowly, watching the gate close behind me. I follow the rough track up and around some trees. To the untrained eye, it looks as though it is just an empty parcel of land, just trees and what looks to be a camping ground where there had once been a fire. It was from one of the contractors who worked on the site. I left it there as I thought it added to the distraction of what the site really is. The only sign of anything being built here was a weathered and dirty slab of concrete, the size of a decent single car garage just sitting in the middle of a cleared section of land. It had been there for years, no sign of being added to. It was as though a shed was planned but was never finished. A big pile of metal framing remains atop the slab, rusting away.

As I get closer to the slab, I take out my binoculars and do a full 360 look around me. Satisfied I'm alone, I get out of the car and walk over to the slab.

'Sarina, activate bunker. Check for intruders.'

A female electronic voice responds, 'Affirmative, checking perimeter and interior zones.' I turn and look around the property, just taking in the view. It's a beautiful spot, quiet and peaceful. A perfect spot for a nice house. A few moments later Sarina responds: 'Perimeter is secure and no suspicious life forms are on the property. The bunker is secure. Do you wish to enter the facility?'

I walk back to the car. 'Yes, prepare for entry.'

As I get back in the driver's seat, the slab starts to move. It lifts about 2 metres high on the end closest to me, revealing an entrance. A concrete ramp leads below. I put the car into gear and start to head towards the entrance. As I do, a small machine exits the bunker; it will clean away the tracks of the car before returning into the depths. It gets to work and it is only a few seconds before it reenters the bunker behind me. I drive down into a room below and park the car off to one side. As the entrance closes, darkness envelops me. There is pure silence, almost like I am in one of those desensitisation pods, laying there in the water, where people go to just hit refresh and disconnect from all the craziness of the world.

The bunker has an almost wet, mossy smell to it that I strangely enjoy. It's a strange sensation, sitting here in darkness, but I don't have to wait long before the bunker starts to come to life. Lights all turn on and a large metal door opens in front of me, revealing a massive room.

The size of a professional basketball court, the bunker has a theatre setup, kitchen, bathroom, even a food storage room. If I needed to stay down here for a few months, I could. Over in the far corner though is the true reason for this place. I have a wall of screens and enough computing power to set my sights on a country if I wanted to. Anything I could need in case something goes wrong. I think it's always best to plan for the worst and when it all works out, then it's a nice surprise.

I take my bag and toss it on the couch. I'll have some breakfast and then get to work. I have some bad guys to torment. I grab some cereal and scoff it down. When I finish, I put the bowl in the sink and make myself a cup of coffee.

'Sarina, initiate hunt protocols.' All the computer systems start to come to life. Sarina is some of my best work. I created her to help keep the bunkers safe and keep them ready for when I need them, but she has become much more than that over the last few years. She is like a sidekick, ready to assist at any moment.

I sit at my desk. It's time to find my next target.

CHAPTER 7

TAKING OUT THE TRASH

My new target's name is Justine Thomas. She's a businesswoman who loans money to people, pays out their debts and gets them back on their feet. That's what she tells them anyway. The loans are under terms no one can afford to pay. After a few months, she repossesses their homes, businesses, everything they have. She sells it to them as wanting to help them, to give them a chance but she never really wants to help anyone, she just wants to take more, steal everything from everyone. Just make everyone else poorer and fill her pockets with everything they had.

She is ruthless, enforcing her control over these people with an army of thugs and enforcers. Many of her victims never had a choice. They didn't want to take the money, they wanted to be left alone, but if they don't eat up her lies about just wanting to help them, her goons make them agree. The police don't get involved because she isn't technically doing anything illegal. They can't prove she forces them under duress to sign the agreements, no witnesses ever come forward.

I have seen a trail of destruction and pain. Families torn apart, all because she wants more money. That's all she cares about. Money.

I do what I normally do. I get access to everything she has, worm my way into her life. I don't change anything, I don't move anything, I just get into position.

I have spent the last 24 hours hacking into her bank accounts, her email, social media accounts—I have everything. Even her poorly hidden millions in an overseas account. Now I need to turn my attention to her company systems. I need to infiltrate the network and see what other secrets she is hiding. Maybe something the police could use against her or at least humiliate this piece of human trash.

I start with a gentle scan of her exterior facing systems. The usual stuff, nothing too exciting. A firewall and some servers sitting behind it. I'll touch softly. I don't want them to know I'm here just yet. I don't want to ruin the surprise. I focus on the firewall and manipulate it to my will by executing several exploits the company hasn't patched. Sometimes they make it too easy for me. Why don't they get the basics right? Instead, they waste their money on fancy blinky light solutions but ignore everything else that would probably keep them safe, well safer maybe. The worst part is, most don't even set up the new systems completely, but leave default passwords or just don't do anything with them.

Why throw all that money away when they aren't even going to try to use it? I work my way through the network trying to escalate my access. It takes me a few more hours before I own the network and everything on it. I can do whatever I want now with nothing being logged. I hide in the shadows, exfiltrating data. I'll have a lot to analyse. Well, Sarina will, before we move to stage two.

Once I have everything in place, I initiate the second stage of my plan. I freeze everything, lock her bank accounts, her credit cards, lines of credit. Everything is locked down. I have Sarina prepare all the data I have collected, ready to send it through to the media and authorities if that is the path I must take. I have a feeling that will be the case, but I want to give her the choice.

They know I'm on the network now. I can see them checking everything; they know something is wrong. I release a ransomware bug into the corporate network and bring it to its knees. I can see it spreading through the network. The security team has seen it, but it is too late; they can't stop it now. It's only minutes before every system is locked out and my nice message is displayed on the screen.

'Your systems are locked. It is worthless trying to unlock them. I have all your backups. I control everything. You should answer that phone, Justine, it is important.'

CHAPTER 8

CHANCE FOR REDEMPTION

'Sarina, put me through to Justine, will you? I think we have a few things to talk about.' Sarina dials Justine on all of her lines at once, her office, her home, her mobile, and even the burner phone she has been using to talk to her thugs. I can see her in her office looking at the screen. She looks at the desk phone and then the burner phone. I'm guessing she is trying to figure out if she should pick it up or not. She lifts the burner phone and hits the button.

'Who is this? Do you know who you are messing with?' I fight back a laugh. I think it is her that doesn't know who she is dealing with. 'Hello, are you there? Are you going to talk to me or are you just trying to play some game?'

I wait a few more moments before I answer.

In a computerised tone, I respond, 'I know exactly who you are, Justine. I know what you do. I know who you truly are and what you value most.' Sarina adjusts my voice to help protect my identity and ensure no one ever records my real voice. I can see Justine looks a little confused on the camera. She hits the mute button on the phone, but of course, it doesn't affect me.

'Are you tracing this bloody call? Find this bastard and kill him,' she says.

Wow, that's a little aggressive. I don't think we will be going down the easy path today.

'That's not a nice thing to say, Justine. You'll hurt my feelings.' She looks at the mute button and it is still on. 'Don't worry about how I can still hear what you said, you have much bigger things to worry about now. You can also tell your goons to stop trying to trace me. They will never find my location unless I want them to.'

For some reason, she feels like she needs to unmute the phone before she speaks again. 'What do you want? Money, is that it? How much do you want?'

Straight to business, okay then.

'I want all of your money. That's what I'll take, if you don't do as I ask.'

She laughs. 'Are you serious? Who the hell do you think you are? I'm not giving you a single cent. I'll just hunt you down and make you pay.'

I don't think she truly gets the big picture yet. I better demonstrate it to her. I initiate control of her machines and change the message displayed on her computer.

'You are not in control here.' I see her read the message on screen and talk to her again through the distorted voice. 'Justine, you need to listen to me now very clearly. You are at a fork in the road. You will get to make this choice once, so think carefully before you answer. Do you understand?'

She looks at the message on the screen again. 'Yes, I understand.'

I wait a few moments before responding, 'Your first option is this: You can walk away now and I'll let you keep enough money to have a humble life, one in which you try to do good deeds, not what you are currently used to. The second option: I take everything and burn your house down around you. It's that simple. Do you want some time to make the choice?'

She looks around her, at her men. Trying to figure out her next move. I can see on the camera feed there is a bit of a heated discussion between what I can only assume is one of her head goons and what looks like a tech guy trying to figure out what the hell is going on. It looks like the tech guy is trying to tell the muscle there isn't anything they can do and they are not taking that so well. I feel a little sorry for the tech guy. At this point, this is not going to be a great day for them.

The expression on Justine's face changes; she looks defiant, angry almost.

'No. I'll choose neither of those options. I don't take orders from anyone. I'll find you and kill you.'

'Okay, I'll take that as option two: you want to do this the hard way. Just remember, I gave you a choice.' I terminate the call. 'Sarina, initiate the move. Take all of the money and wash it. Make it untraceable.' I intertwine my fingers, flexing them backwards and hearing my knuckles crack. Time to get to work. I load up my systems, initiate my takedown platforms and initiate a full systems burnout. My programs are designed to overheat a system and make them catch alight. I stole the move from another hacker. I don't know their name, but they did this move on some crime syndicate systems and literally burned the house down, exactly what I want to achieve here.

That hacker is a badass, but I haven't been able to find anything on them. Anyway, that's a puzzle for another time. Right now, I need to focus on Justine. I initiate the takedown of her shadow systems as well, her money laundering, everything. There is going to be nothing left. No records of money owed to her, nothing. A few minutes go by and I can see her workstation burst into flames. She jumps back and shouts all sorts of profanities at her goons. The alarms go off in the building and I can see a similar action taking place on all systems.

This move is so cool, I'll have to thank that hacker someday. I'm not finished though. I send off the files to the Australian Federal Police and all the different media outlets. It will be only a few minutes and she will be on every television station.

I clean my tracks and finish burning all the systems as I go. I make one final call.

'I told you that you might regret your decision. Turn over a new leaf. Be better, or I'll return.' I don't give her a chance to reply, I initiate burnout on the phones as well. I see her throw it as it gets hot and her men do the same, the devices exploding into flames shortly afterwards. I wait as the federal police arrive moments later and handcuff Justine. I think her whole team will be spending some time inside.

The building is *actually* burning down. Okay, maybe that move is a little too badass. I guess it's one way to ensure there is no evidence of my involvement. I initiate the final procedure on the security systems and see my connection severed as I do. I'll have to watch the news for any further updates on this one.

I'll sit it out here with a few movies before I head back to Jacob's life tomorrow.

A job well done.

CHAPTER 9

BACK TO THE REAL WORLD

I get up early and prep for leaving the bunker. I have Sarina scan the perimeter and initiate exit mode. I get in the car and prepare to leave the bunker.

'Exit mode initiation has been aborted. There is someone on the property. I'm initiating analysis and determining the risk to the facility,' Sarina says.

I jump back out of the car and head inside. Maybe Justine was smarter than I thought, maybe she found me. I return to my desk chair and scan the cameras.

'Where are they?'

One of the camera's views is enlarged on the main monitor.

'It would appear to be a minimal threat, a hunter of sorts, trespassing on your land.' I watch them walk through the land, walking over the very top of the entrance to the bunker. They look to be in their mid-50s, reasonably fit, with a particularly well maintained grey beard. They look like someone who looks after themselves. Their clothes look like they are very well worn, something they have had for years.

I see them take aim at a few kangaroos with their rifle. They are not a very good shot; they completely miss their target. After about an hour of chasing off the only wild animals on the property, without actually hitting any of them, they leave the way they came.

To be on the safe side, I wait it out for another thirty minutes or so before I direct a rescan of the property.

'Facility is all clear, reinitiating exit mode. Lockdown will initiate on your exit of the property.' I jump back in my car and see the bunker door open. I turn the car around and head back up the ramp. As I exit, the same machine follows me out, clearing my tracks from the facility. Once it returns, the slab settles back down into place, like it never moved. The gate to the property is already open when I reach it and it closes as I drive through. The facility will be in lockdown now until my return.

I head back into town and it seems like it never changes. The same people always doing the same things. People always working. If any of them knew what I just did, would they cheer me on or would they condemn me for it? I don't know. I don't do it for anyone else though, it's mainly for me. I feel better for a few weeks after I take down someone like Justine, someone who deserves it. I guess one day I'll get caught and then they can judge me. Until then, this is me, this is what I do.

Now it's back to the world of Jacob, back to the house and back to the party life. I park in the driveway and head inside. My housemates are getting dressed up.

'Hurry up Jacob, you are coming with us. Let's get our party on,' Steve says.

I'm not really in the mood, but I just go with it. I get ready and we head out to some seedy club in the valley. I've never been here before. I really am not into the clubbing scene, but I just sit back and try to enjoy the night. I think I have earned it.

I sit in the back corner of the club, watching everyone dancing and drinking. The hours go past with a blur. I have no idea how long I have been here. I don't even know how many beers I have had. I have probably had a little too much to drink, but I'm still able to function as normal. I should have stayed home.

I can see one of my roommates, Tim, throwing up all over the floor on the other side of the room. I think that's our cue to leave. The bouncers grab Tim and haul him towards the door. Steve is only a few steps behind, he sees it's time to leave as well.

We all pile in an Uber and head back home. The sun is coming up and we've been out all night. Just perfect. Classes with a hangover and no sleep.

CHAPTER 10

OFFLOAD THE CASH

It's been a couple of weeks since the last job. Sarina has washed the money and it's ready to be offloaded. I have a sequence configured in a custom app on my burner phone to process the transactions. I transfer most of the money to charities, anonymous donations, and then about 10% goes to me for expenses. It is still a lot of money. I know I'm getting rich off taking down these people. Yes, they are scum, but am I much better? Some days I'm not sure if I am, but the charity donations make me feel better about myself. Makes me feel like the hero of my story, not the villain, but I must be a dark hero. One of those shadowy ones where it's hard to tell whether they're good or bad, they don't even know themselves, most of the time. I think that's more like me.

I head to a café in one of the outlying suburbs. I have a baseball cap on and sunglasses. I have scoped out this place. I know where all the cameras are and I have already gained access to the WiFi, so it will just auto-connect when I walk in. I'll go in, order a coffee, pay for it with cash, and execute the money transfers on my phone while I'm there. In and out in a few minutes, with no trace of who I am, what I did, or why I was there.

I pull up, down the street from the cafe, at the end where no cameras are watching. I always try to keep as low a footprint as possible, but I need to be even more careful in this situation, just in case someone picks up on the transfers and goes looking for where they came from. I get out of the car and lock it. I don my cap and adjust the sunglasses. I'm good to go.

I walk down the street, aware I'm across the road from an ATM. I turn my head towards the windows of the shops to my right, not enough to give a clear reflection, but enough to make it impossible to get a clear view of my face from the camera on that ATM. I continue down the street and lower my head so my face is shielded by the cap from the camera up ahead on the street. I continue past the pole and look to the left, so the camera in the shop front can't get my face either.

I get to the front of the café and enter near the front left of the door. I chose this angle as it's the best way to give a bad angle of me in the shop's surveillance. I can't avoid them completely, but it will help me reduce the coverage and it all counts. I wait in the shadows until I'm called up to the counter to make my order, looking towards the front of the store as I do, to hide my face. Once the order is placed, I step back into the shadows.

I glance around the café. A girl in the corner taps away on her laptop and some other people scroll their phones. All of them are probably students, taking advantage of the free WiFi. I access the phone in my pocket and check it is connected to the WiFi, it is. I do one more quick look around and initiate the process; it should only take a minute. I feel my phone vibrate. The first sequence is done. I'm about to initiate the second final sequence when the barista calls out my number.

I step forward, and look towards the front of the shop, as before. As I approach the counter, I pull the phone out slightly to check its status. It's ready to go for the second process. I click the button to initiate and I see the code run over the screen. I lock it and put it back in my pocket. A few seconds later, it vibrates again. Done. Cash has been moved and charity payments have been completed.

I pull out some cash to pay the guy behind the counter. As I take my coffee, he tells me they can't take cash at the moment, something wrong with the till. Crap, what do I do now? I can't use EFTPOS. I can't leave something I can be traced with. Then I remember I have a few of those gift card visas I use for things I need to buy for work. It's hard to trace them and I can order them online with a different identity that isn't linked to Jacob or Shadow. I pull out my wallet, ensuring I keep my current ID facing the opposite way to the cameras. It would be embarrassing if that's how I got caught.

I tap the card on the EFTPOS machine and the coffee is paid for and the crisis is averted. I almost had to walk out without my coffee, now that would have sucked. The instant crap my housemates insist on buying is like drinking out of an ashtray.

I take the coffee and make my way out of the shop and back towards where the car is parked, ensuring I complete my earlier manoeuvres in reverse order to avoid the cameras. I see some girls taking selfies up ahead with a flashy sports car. I can't get out of the way and avoid the other cameras. I think they may have my face in their selfie. Hopefully, it's a bad angle and the cap helps cover my face.

I reach the car and climb in, removing my hat and glasses. I sip my coffee. The hassle was worth the effort just for the coffee. Time to get out of here.

CHAPTER 11

POLITICAL UNREST

I'm back at the bunker again. I've found myself a new target. A politician, a very powerful man with some very powerful friends. I don't know if this one will give me some heat from the feds but this guy, Malcolm Wade is doing something shady and I'm going to find out what it is and tell the world about it. This one isn't about money; this one is about power.

He will walk over anyone who gets in his way. He doesn't care who he has to hurt, but he does it all with a smile on his face and clean as a whistle reputation. I know he is dirty and I'll show everyone else he is as well. I'll take all his power and all the money. I'll give all the money to charity. I still have more than enough from the last job, this is just about teaching this guy that he should be acting in the best interest of the public, not himself.

I have been spreading my control through his life. It won't be long now before I have access to his entire digital footprint. His social accounts, banks, emails, and cloud storage for his files.

I can see he has been using his privilege as a member of parliament to do shady real-estate deals. He buys the property cheap and then works secret deals to put highways or tunnels there. To which he then sells the previously worthless land to developers and the government for billions. It's a great money earner, this one, and admittedly is very clever of Malcolm, but this type of corruption is forbidden. Parliamentary members can't use their positions for their gain.

That's not the worst of it though, the guy also takes advantage of young beautiful women who come to work in his office. He has secret recordings of him forcing himself on these young women, using his position of power to get what he wants. The girls are too scared to do anything about it, so he gets away with being a monster. His whole office probably needs to be disinfected.

Most of them don't resist his advances. I guess they're using what they have to gain an advantage and probably think they can get it by giving him what he wants. Some of them though, it's clear they aren't into it and he forces himself on them, rapes them. You can tell from the recordings they don't want it to happen. There's no audio but the body language alone is clear. He rips at their clothing, taking what he wants with absolutely no regard for their consent. I can feel the anger build as I find more and more evidence of his wrongdoings.

People like this should rot in jail for life; there should be no quick escape. Just a long, painful existence to remember why they're imprisoned.

One of the girls left his office with a bloody lip from when he hit her and jammed her head hard down onto his desk, before forcing himself on her.

This guy is going down. I'll make sure of it. The hush money I see he has paid most of them, is not enough in my book. They deserve better.

I have Sarina anonymise the girls and I post the videos to all of his social accounts. I post them to all of the government social sites and to the media outlets. All over the world too. Not just in Australia, but everywhere. I want everyone to know what this scum bag did. I send unedited versions of the videos to the AFP and all the records about his dodgy deals too. I don't think it will be long before he gets a knock at his door.

I just hope this doesn't dredge up too many painful memories for these women. I don't want to inflict any more pain on them but Malcolm needs to pay. Now all that's left is his money. I think this time I'll give the money to a domestic violence and women's health charity. I think it's appropriate he gets to fund a charity to help women deal with monsters like him for the next ten years. Very fitting.

I need to ensure I clean my tracks on this one. He'll still have friends in high places who will come after me for this, maybe they even are part of this whole club which treats women like this. I'll need to dig deeper to find others like him and put their dirty laundry out for all to see. It is worth the risk to make sure this type of behaviour is put to an end.

It's time to watch the news and watch the minister be thrown under a proverbial bus by everyone. No one will want to be seen as a supporter of him. He will be alone. Some may help him in the shadows, but in public view, he will be on his own. I switch on the TV and he is already starting to appear on every channel. Enjoy the attention arsehole, you deserve it.

CHAPTER 12

BACKLASH

I have seen a bit of chatter since I burned the politician a few weeks ago. It looks like I pissed some powerful people off. People are looking for who did it, trying to get someone to gloat about it. It's a trap, one I'm not going to fall for. No one is talking though. The shadows are quiet. Many suspect it is me, but I don't think any of them would want to even suggest my name or are stupid enough to get involved.

Attacking a politician is not the smartest thing to do as a hacker. A lot of them may not be super-tech savvy, but they do have money and connections. They'll do anything to try and find me. Malcolm certainly fits that category. I don't know how he is paying for it though, maybe it's just someone who doesn't want me to keep digging into politicians' activities. Maybe someone else has secrets they would prefer didn't get laid out for the world to see. Makes sense, I guess. It does make me curious though, what they have to hide. I just might have to find out.

I think I should go dark for a few weeks though, until all of this dies down a little. I haven't been to the bunker since the attack and will keep it that way for a while longer. I better get used to the fun life of Jacob. I'll be stuck in it for a while.

I head home. I'll just hang out there. Hopefully, the guys aren't up to too many shenanigans. I pull up in the driveway and make my way inside. As I do, I walk in on the boys sitting in the lounge room with porn blaring at almost full volume. I don't know what the hell I'm seeing right now, but this shit ain't normal.

'Bloody hell guys, do you need to watch that crap in the lounge room? Seriously, that stuff is weird.' They just look at me as though I'm an alien or something.

'Dude, just chill. Sit down and watch some with us, it's some hardcore stuff.' I just shake my head and keep walking through the lounge room and into my room.

I can still hear the moaning and groaning. I can only imagine what the neighbours think. I don't know why I helped these guys set up the porn site, all they ever do now is watch that stuff. They say they are just product testing, but I think they get off on that weird arse stuff they list on their site. The site does pay for their lifestyle though, so I guess there's that. A win-win for them. They get weird porn to satisfy their desires, and an income to support their rent, food, and partying.

I grab my headphones. It's time to cancel out that, whatever *that* is they are watching. I settle in with a movie on my laptop. Time to let everything else melt away.

CHAPTER 13

RUINED

Tick, tick, tick. The near silence is almost deafening. I have been sitting here for hours and I cannot figure out how I got here. Not to this place, I'm still in my house after all, the kitchen to be specific, but in this situation. I'd been watching a movie when suddenly a bunch of burly men in dark uniforms stormed my room and hauled me out. Now they're in there, searching for something.

I just don't understand where it all went wrong. Was it one choice or was it a set of decisions that made this path a reality? Could I have changed my fate or was this always where I was going to end up?

The metal around my wrist is starting to dig in. The fed that put the cuffs on me was young. To be honest, I don't think he looked like he was old enough to have finished high school, let alone be an AFP officer. I guess that means I'm starting to get old since almost all of the feds in my house seem like they are a little older than middle graders. Yep, I'm the old guy in the room, and I'm not even twenty-one yet.

I think he thought I was going to try to escape, or it was the first time he had ever put cuffs on a real suspect. If it was indeed his first time, he has done a pretty good job. These things are not going anywhere and I guess neither am I, unless this bunch decide they have made a massive mistake and just let me go. I don't see that happening. Well, at least not yet anyway. They think they have me right where they want me.

I look up and see a girl walk in. She is different to the others. She looks like she belongs in a rom-com or something, not hanging out with these feds. She is a little more casually dressed, extremely pretty, and has this look of intelligence about her. There is something about her that puzzles me. I don't know what it is, I just can't put my finger on it. I can't help but stare. We connect eyes as she gets closer. She holds my gaze for what feels like forever; there is a fire in her eyes. She is strong, of that I'm certain. There's no fear, no doubt in her eyes. She is absorbing every detail of me, her surroundings, everything. I can immediately tell she's the only one in this room who could be a threat to me.

Is she the one who found me? Did I make a mistake? Did I forget to clean something up? It just doesn't make any sense; I am always careful. I am not sure I will ever know what it was that gave me away, maybe I just got sloppy, too arrogant, thinking I was untouchable.

Stupid.

She turns towards some of the other feds and starts to help them look through my stuff. Through the doorway into my room, I can see them collecting up the multitude of electronic devices and tagging everything. They are certainly ensuring chain of custody is maintained. I guess if they truly do have me, which they don't, but if they do, then I'm not getting off on a technicality, that's for sure.

If only they knew this was a complete waste of their time. They won't find a single trace of evidence on any of these devices. If they are lucky, they might find some porn or torrents from my housemates they might be able to charge them for—those boys get up to some funky stuff. I can only imagine what they get up to on the net. I tend to avoid looking at anything they do. These AFP stooges are going to have some fun dredging through all of that history. Hopefully, that girl doesn't have that job, I don't like the idea of her having to sift through all of that.

I have a feeling that isn't what they are looking for though. I have a bad feeling they are here for me. I have been isolated from my housemates since they arrived. I am the target not them. But why? Have they linked me to the recent attack on Australian politician, and terrible human being, Malcom? They haven't told me anything yet, so I am only making assumptions.

If they do think that, they are exactly right, but they have no proof and they won't find any here. Maybe it was the money I took from his accounts they are pissed about. I took millions, so what. It's still chump change in the grand scheme of things.

It was probably the rape videos I shared on all the social sites and sent to the media. That's probably what it is. You can't come back from that sort of thing as a politician. I'm not sorry I did it though. That scum bag needed to be thrown out into the street for everyone to see who he is. I'm certain many of the people in this room, if not all, probably agree with what I did, but their job is to catch me. I get that, I do.

Tick, tick, tick. That bloody clock is driving me crazy. How much longer do I need to sit here, while they rummage through my things? This is seriously frustrating. It would be simpler if I could just tell them they aren't going to find a thing. This isn't where I work. It's not even in the same fifty km radius, but we will just have to let the theatrics continue. I'll need to keep a low profile for a while until I can slip away and take a flight out of here. I already have access to the fed's systems, so it will be easy to swap out my details for another's, but I'll have to wait for a few weeks before the details of my life as Jacob are a little fuzzy in the minds of anyone in this room, replace it with someone that looks similar and that will be enough to get them off my back.

It's strange what thoughts flow through your mind when you are completely fixed in a situation like this, with no way of entertaining yourself. It's good to disconnect though, bounce around in my head for a while. My perfect Sunday roast is starting to burn, I can smell it. I was looking forward to eating that pork crackling.

'Hey you, get my roast out of the oven. Hey, it is starting to burn.' The fed doesn't respond but gets it out of the oven, and plonks it down on the sink. It looks like I did a perfect job on the crackling too. Typical, I finally nail the crackle and it is sitting on the bench going cold. My mouth waters just thinking about it, but sadly I don't think I'll be getting something to eat for a while. These guys look like they are just starting to settle in.

I'm confident they aren't going to find anything to pin any of this stuff on me. I have been careful. Unless they have found the bunker, they are going to have to cut me loose at some point. Even if they don't, it won't matter. In another few days, the systems are designed to self-erase and burn themselves. Maybe they have found the bunker? Nah, that isn't possible. I have been careful. I guess it doesn't matter even if they do, I couldn't even crack my encryption, so I'm sure they won't even get close without setting off defences. Sarina will destroy the complex before she allows them to take anything.

Do they know who they are dealing with? What I'm capable of? It's doubtful. I know I'm not the good guy in this story. I profit from bringing down these leaches. It's the charities and the volunteers for these organisations who are the good ones. The donations are my way of feeling a little better about myself and the targets are always people that deserve it. But maybe it is my turn. Maybe this is the end of the line for me, maybe I have finally been caught. Nah, I don't think any of these people are smart enough to have caught me out. Except maybe that girl. Who is she? I guess I'll just have to sit here in my thoughts, waiting to see what it is they think they know about me.

Tick, tick, tick.

Grrrr. I swear when they let me go, I'm going to smash the hell out of that clock. It's like a sledgehammer just smashing away at my skull. This is going to be a long night.

'Hey, you in the glasses, yes, you. How about cutting me a few slices of that pork over there?' Wow. I just got a look that very clearly says I'm not getting any of that food tonight. I might as well just admit to myself I'm not going anywhere for now. I may as well get some sleep. I'm sure they will wake me up when I start to snore, or they are ready to go. Either way, I think it's time for some shut-eye for me to get the hell out of my head.

CHAPTER 14

INTERROGATION

I don't know what time they finished at the house, but it was late. When they woke me up to be taken away, I had been asleep a while. I had a bit of drool on my face. Charming. I hope that girl didn't see that. I don't know why I care what she thinks. I need to focus. They put some sort of bag over my head and took me to some hidden facility. I don't know where it is. I tried to keep track of the turns but I think they may have been going around in circles. It was probably deliberate, to throw me off track. To my frustration, it worked. I have no idea where I am. We might be underground, but it is just a guess.

They put me in an interrogation room. I have been here for maybe seven or eight hours, it's hard to tell. It could be just two or it could be twenty; I have no frame of reference. They have been asking me question after question about how I hacked into the politician's systems, what I did with the money, and if Jacob is my real name. It is like a loop; it just keeps going.

'Jacob, are you listening to me?' Here we go again, round number 53, give or take a few. 'I'm talking to you, Jacob. Tell me why you hacked the senator. What access do you have? Have you gained access to any other political systems?'

I guess with this continued line of questioning, we know who is pulling the strings. Politicians are understandably a little uneasy about having their secrets spilled. I guess it means they have more to hide. That doesn't surprise me at all, they are politicians after all.

'Look, I don't know who you all are. Some sort of police, I'm guessing. I don't know where it is you have taken me but I don't know anything about this hacking business you keep talking about. I can barely figure out how to download pirated movies. How in the hell could I access a senator's private files? I'm just a uni student, trying to have a good time. If this is about all that weird porn, I can explain.'

My interrogator leans a little closer to me. 'Jacob, we don't care about that weird arse porn your housemates are into. None of that is illegal. We want to know about your hacking activities. We know you are Shadow. We know you are responsible and it is only a matter of time before we find the evidence we need to prove it. Why don't you drop this act of yours and tell us the truth?'

So they know I'm Shadow. Hey, that's the first time I have heard them use the name, that may have been a slip-up. A chill runs down my spine.

'I have already told you hundreds of times, I don't know anything about the hacking stuff. It doesn't matter how many times you keep asking me, my answer is still going to be the same. It's the truth. When am I going to get a lawyer, shouldn't I get a lawyer?'

He bangs his hand down on the table. 'Stop wasting our time Jacob, we know who you are. Drop the stupid act.' He gets up out of his chair and makes his way around the table and sits down on the table next to me 'You don't get a lawyer. You are to be charged with treason, cyber terrorism. You can be held for as long as we like until you tell us what we want to know.'

I know that's a lie. I might not be able to get a lawyer due to the suspected attack I carried out on the federal politician but I know unless they have proof, they will need to let me go. I just need to last out that time. Once I'm released, they'll watch me and I'll need to be very careful until I get a chance to slip my tail. The opportunity will come up though. When they settle in and relax, I can react. I just need to be patient.

'Hey, can someone get me something to eat? I think it would be against the law to hold me with no food or water. You owe me that at least, after wasting my perfectly cooked roast dinner.'

One of them looks at the two-way mirror, I assume to seek permission.

It only takes a few minutes before someone knocks on the door. One of the interrogators opens it and is handed a sandwich, a vending machine snack bar, plus a bottle of water.

'Looks like someone agreed with you.' I take the food the agent holds out and eat slowly, helping drag out the time until they start my interrogation loop again. I know they are wearing down. They'll need to call it quits soon. I can outlast them. I know I can. Just stick to the same story and it will all work out.

I sit there for a few more minutes before I decide to have a bit of fun.

'Hey officer, I know you all think I'm some hacker guy called… what did you call them? Oh, that's right, *Shadow*. Look, I'm not him. But I was wondering, once all this is over, is there any chance you could get me that spunky tech chick's name and number? You know, the girl at my house during the raid? I'd like to take her out on a date. Can you ask her for me?' The cops laugh.

'Dream on kid, that ain't ever gonna happen. Just eat your food and worry about telling us the truth. Everything you know.'

'This is going nowhere for any of us. Can we move on already?'

We go on the loop again a few more times when I hear a knock on the back of the mirror. Hopefully, they have finally given up. One of them exits the room while the other stands in the corner with his arms crossed, staring at me. Good thing I'm already in an interrogation room or I might think I'm in trouble with the way he is looking at me.

CHAPTER 15

APOLOGY

It took about an hour before the interrogator returned to the room, but at least the other guy just let me be. I don't know what they were doing but it looks like we are ready to go again.

'Look kid, your time is up. I don't have much time left with you before they take you off and throw you in some hole somewhere. Let me help you. Tell me something I can use.' He sits back in his chair across from me and just waits for me to respond.

'I don't know anything. I can't give you what you want. They can't really throw me in a dark hole, can they? I'm innocent.' He clears his throat, getting ready for a response when there is another knock at the door. He gets up and leaves the room. Returning after what seems like only a few minutes, he heads back over to the desk and sits down with me again, but this time it would appear his mood has softened a little.

'It looks like it is your lucky day. Someone out there thinks you are telling the truth. Let me be clear Jacob, I think you are a lying bastard, but I don't make the rules around here, I just follow them. You are being released. It will be an hour or so before the paperwork is finalised and your ride out of here will be ready. So sit tight, someone will come to get you when you are good to go.' He turns and gets up out of his chair. 'I hope there are no hard feelings about all of this, I was just doing my job.'

I shake my head. 'No, no hard feelings. I know you were doing your job. I hope you catch this Shadow.' I think I hit a bit of a nerve with that comment.

The man's face darkens and he leans over the table again. 'You listen to me. I know you are the person we are looking for. I can't prove it now but we will. Don't go anywhere Jacob, we will be watching you very closely. Very closely indeed.' I don't respond to his statement. I already knew that, but there's nothing to gain from pissing them off more. I just lean back in my chair and wait for the time to drift by until my ride out of here finally turns up.

Another hour goes past and someone official looking comes into the room and sits down across from me. Please tell me we are not going to start that whole demented loop again.

'Sorry for keeping you waiting, Mr Loxley. Jacob, isn't it? Do you mind if I call you Jacob?'

I shake my head. 'No, I don't mind. Jacob will be fine.'

'I would like to formally apologise for the inconvenience this whole ordeal has caused you and I would like to help you sort out your release paperwork.' She takes a document from the manila folder she has in front of her and hands me a pen. 'Please sign this and we can get you all organised to get out of here.' I look over the prisoner release form. I sign it and hand it back to her with the pen. 'Great. Now that is all done, let me see about getting you out of here.'

She leaves the room, the heavy door clanging behind her.

CHAPTER 16

CATCH AND RELEASE

A few minutes go by before the door to the interrogation room opens yet again. This time it's four swat guys all in black. They split the group in the middle and walk around either side of the table until I'm surrounded.

'Please get to your feet, Sir.' I do as directed and one of them pulls the chair away. The one on my right turns me towards him and secures a set of cuffs on both my hands and feet. Those you see in movies all the time, where it looks impossible to walk in due to the ten cm length of chain between your feet. I get it. It's so a prisoner can't run.

He does them up tight enough so they dig into the skin around my ankles. I resist the urge to flinch as he does them up and my skin is pinched. A black bag is thrown over my head and a drawstring at the bottom is pulled so there is no gap between the bag and my neck. I know it's to stop me from seeing anything from any angle, but it's probably a little overkill.

'You have been secured and you will now be escorted out of these facilities. You will do exactly as directed. If you do not do as directed, one of my team here will strike you. Do you understand?' Oh wow, these guys are serious. WHACK... My breath wooshes out of my lungs as I receive a blow to the ribs. That is going to leave a mark. 'Do you understand what I have just told you?'

I wait a few seconds risking a second hit, why I let the pain of the first strike pass. 'Yes, I understand. I don't do as I'm told, you hurt me, yep got it.'

'If you try to run or strike out at my team, you may be shot. Do not mess with us. Do you understand?'

To ensure I don't get another hit in the ribs I answer immediately.

'Yes, I understand. Pain and death high possibility if I mess around or do anything you deem stupid. Yep, got that.' Rough hands grab my elbow from either side and they pull me forward just a little faster than is reasonable in these chains and I nearly fall but they keep me up and slightly slow their pace while I slowly shuffle my feet in the direction they are pulling me. I assume out of the room and back to the elevator, but I was blindfolded on the way in as well, so I can't know for sure.

Panic flutters in my chest. What if they're taking me to that black hole somewhere and that document I signed earlier wasn't really a release form? What if I signed away my freedom by mistake? That would certainly put a ripple in my life plans. Well, I guess it would if I had any real life plans. I must have been dragging my feet as I feel a sudden sharp pain in my ribs, on the opposite side this time. I groan. At least they are evening it up. I try and steady my breathing. Gees, if this is how they handle someone they are supposedly releasing, I wouldn't want to be someone they are locking up for good.

I try to walk as quickly as they'd like, but it's awkward to say the least, with this chain between my ankles. Don't get distracted. I don't want another hit. It will be what it will be and I'll just figure it out. I hear the elevator doors open and they basically drag me into it and spin me around to face back the way I came. The elevator starts to move. It feels as though we are going up, not down, but

I could just be disorientated. It doesn't matter. I don't plan to ever come back to this place, wherever it is. The elevator stops. I'm pulled out again a little aggressively and allowed to shuffle in the forward direction again.

I hear the car door open in front of me and one of the guys helps me in. I get pulled from the other side, I assume to the middle of the seat. I can feel one of them slide in on either side next to me before the car is started and we appear to be moving. It's weird I know but for a moment when the car first started to move it felt like the car was in an elevator, but that doesn't make any sense at all. I must be imagining it. As we drive along, hopefully to my place, I realise I don't even know what time it is. It could be the middle of the night, for all I know. What happened to Steve and Tim? Have they been released? Did they go through what I did or was it just me who had the pleasure of all that attention?

I wonder if I'll ever see that tech girl again. I hope so, but in a different environment when I'm not the criminal handcuffed to the desk would be nice. Not that I would have a chance with someone like her. Even if I wasn't a criminal, she looks like a girl who knows what she wants and usually gets it. I am not sure she would be interested in me. I'm certainly nothing super special. I wouldn't say I'm an ugly guy, but I would certainly have to pull out the big guns to impress her. Wow, I'm hung up on this girl. Why am I so infatuated with her? No one has held my attention like her. What is it about her…?

I picture her in my mind. She is something. That intelligence in her eyes, the fire I can see in her and the aura of confidence is intoxicating. I can feel it, even now after days have passed. Is my mind playing tricks on me, making her into something much more than she is? I need to find her, know who she is, not the surface crap, but who she is deep down. I'll keep that thought for another time.

Right now, I need to figure out if this is going to end well for me.

We continue driving for nearly an hour. Probably more to cause confusion than anything else, but suddenly we come to a stop. Here we go. I hear the door open and the one on my right closes with a bit too much force. These gym junkies don't know their own strength. Woop, one of them grabs me and almost yanks me out of the car. I guess this is my stop. I can feel them undoing the chains around my legs and then my hands. The last thing to come off is the head cover. As it's removed, I'm hit with the glare of the sun. It makes my eyes water and I withdraw from it for a moment. As my eyes adjust, I can see the sun is low in the sky above my house, which means it is early morning.

'You are free to go, Mr Loxley, but I was told to ensure you understand we will be watching you. Do not attempt to leave the country or even the city or we will place you back under arrest as a flight risk until we get to the bottom of all this. Do you understand, or would you like a reminder?'

Oh, hell no. I don't want another bruise on my ribs. 'Yes, I understand. Don't leave town, we will be watching. Affirmative.' He seems to be happy with that response. They all climb back into the car and drive off. As they do, I see a van parked down the street. I guess that is one of my watchers. I wave at the van, for no real reason. I know I won't get a response but thought I would let them know I see them.

The street is quiet and I can hear music coming from inside the house. I make my way inside and as I enter the lounge, I'm almost knocked over backwards by my housemates.

'You've been gone for days. We didn't know if they would ever let you go. What did you say to piss them off so much? They let us go after a few hours,' Tim says, slapping me on the shoulder. I wait until they get off me before I answer.

'I don't know. They kept asking about your porn collection. Maybe they were trying to figure out how to get a subscription, or maybe it was because I asked them for the hot fed's number. I don't think they liked that very much.' They both cracked up laughing and Steve went to hand me a beer. 'Guys, it's too early in the morning.' They don't answer me, just offer the beer again. 'No thanks. I'm going to get some sleep before they decide to come back.'

CHAPTER 17

LIVE THE LIE

The last two weeks have gone past in a blur, almost like when you wake up from a dream and it is only partially in your mind. It's foggy and you don't feel you have experienced it but you just can't tell what is reality yet. You are trying to shake off the fog of sleep, but it lingers and clings to your mind. That's been my existence since they dropped me back at my door almost two weeks ago.

I have been just living the lie, the lie of Jacob Loxley. I'm going to classes probably more than I ever have before, hanging out with the boys, and admittedly drinking probably a little too much. At least, that is what I'm letting everyone believe. Especially my watchers. I can feel their eyes on me constantly. I think they even have bugs in my house, maybe hidden surveillance cameras too, but I'm trying to ignore them. I need to live this lie until they all believe it. If I keep going though, I might believe it myself soon.

I'm at another party tonight with the guys. It's the usual frat type scenario, too much alcohol and way too many public displays of affection from couples in almost every direction. It is almost sickening really. I hate how people think it's cool to dry hump out in the open for all to see. Seriously people, get a room. No one needs to see that stuff. I get it, you drink too much, your inhibitions fall to the wayside, and you let your urges take control. The feeling of just letting go, going with the moment, feeling your body mould with someone else. The electricity of the whole scenario would be enough to excite anyone, but even if it makes me old fashioned in the eyes of my peers, I still think there is a time and place for all of that.

I catch a glimpse of a girl walking past the back window. She looks in my direction and for a split second, it's like I'm looking at that girl from the feds, the one who keeps lingering in my mind. It's not really her, but I let my mind run with thoughts of her. She has been on my mind quite a bit over the last few weeks. I'm a little infatuated. She clouds my thoughts with almost everything I do. Her eyes, her lips, I just can't shake her from my mind. It is dangerous. I should forget about her, pretend as though she never existed. Wait for my opportunity and just vanish, but I don't know if that is something I can do. I need to satisfy my curiosity. Maybe once I find out who she is, then I'll be able to let it go and walk away. I need to solve her puzzle, figure out who she is, what makes her tick.

There's a couple across the other side of the room who keeps watching me and talking among themselves. I think they could be part of my surveillance team. They look just a little too old to be part of this scene, maybe in their mid-twenties. The girl has a bulge just under her jacket, near her lower back, which I assume is a gun or she is hiding something else there. I don't see any signs the guy is packing but I would assume he has a weapon somewhere. I don't know if I'm just being paranoid or if the threat is real. It is getting harder to tell. I should probably lay off the beer, three is enough. I'll rinse the bottle and refill it with water in the bathroom to keep up appearances.

I can see the boys up to their usual tricks; they are trying to chat up some pretty girls just outside, near the pool. I should head out there and get in on the conversation. It will look good for those two over there. I'm making my way over to the door leading outside when the girl from the couple who has been watching me breaks off from the guy and heads towards the back door. It's like she is trying to intercept me. What is going to happen? I glance around the room and don't see anyone else moving towards me. The guy she was with is just watching her walk over. When I look back towards where she should be, I startle; she is right in front of me.

I stop in my tracks, like a deer caught in the headlights. I'm dazed, shocked, almost scared, if I'm honest. She takes a step forward and gets in close, her hands run over my abs and slide around my waist. I'm frozen. I look over towards the guy and he is just watching, almost like he is enjoying watching me squirm. Her hand slides down to my backside and lightly squeezes.

'We have been watching you. We both think you are really hot.' Hang on, did she just say *we*? Okay, now I'm lost, what the hell is happening? 'Do you find me attractive?' Her voice is soft and sultry. She is very attractive, that is for sure, but that muscle mountain over there looks like he could crush me with his bare hands. I don't answer the question.

She's undeterred, tilting her head as she continues to touch my chest. 'We would like you to join us tonight for some fun back at our place. Just the three of us, some wine, and quite a lot less clothing. What do you say? Are you in?'

As tempting and fascinating as that could be, that's a *hell no*. She presses her body against mine and leans in to get a little more intimate with me but I stop her.

'Look, I appreciate the offer. You are seriously hot and I'm flattered, but I'm not interested.' She looks puzzled. I assume she doesn't get told no very often. She goes to double down and lean back in. I stop her again.

'You don't want me? Have you seen how I look?' Her lips have fallen into a pout. Okay, she's not happy I'm saying no. Hopefully muscle mountain doesn't get involved, I think that would be bad news for me.

'Look, I'm sorry, I'm just not into the couple's games stuff. You will have to find someone else tonight.' I step around her and make my way outside to the boys, who appear to have been watching the interaction.

'What was that? Was she hitting on you with her man watching? Epic dude.' I turn back to look at her. She is still standing there, arms folded over her chest.

'Yeah, I think she wanted me to join her and the muscle man. I think that was a bit too dangerous for me. What if he changed his mind while I'm having sex with his girl?'

They both look over at him and back at the girl. 'You are probably right, but damn she is hot. A missed opportunity there, Jacob.'

'A missed opportunity to spend a week in the hospital, yeah definitely. Now, why don't you introduce me to your new friends?' I say, smiling at the girls who are standing nearby. 'They are too good for you two idiots.' The guys laugh and introduce me to the girls, Jen and Chloe. I sit down next to one of them. The couple seems to have gotten over my rejection and are moving on, hunting for their next victim or winner. I guess it will depend on how you look at it. I think I dodged a bullet myself. I think the girl is more into the idea than he is, maybe he has to share her with a guy to get her to share with a girl or some sort of trade-off. Maybe he just likes guys and girls, who knows. Not something I'm going to find out personally anyway.

I really hope all this effort I am putting in for the feds is worth it. This normal university student vibe I am trying to put out takes energy, but I need to stay steadfast and keep up appearances just a little bit longer.

A couple more hours go by and the crowd starts to thin. The couple did find their participant and disappeared a while back with them in toe. I hope it plays out well for them and they don't end up in a body bag. I still think it was a gun the girl was carrying, so if they are not cops then I don't think I would like to be heading off alone with them.

I think it is time for me to call it a night. The boys are pairing off with some of the girls and left me to entertain the two remaining girls who don't seem to mind my company.

'Would you two ladies like me to walk you home or escort you to your ride?'

They whisper between themselves for a moment.

'Sure. We'll just check with the other two girls what they are going to do and then get an Uber. If you would wait with us until the Uber arrives, that would be great.' I nod and they both head over and interrupt whatever it is the other two girls are doing over in the dark corner. After a few moments, all four girls come back over, my housemates with them.

'It looks like we are all going to crash at your place tonight, Jacob,' Chloe says.

I nod. 'Okay. Have you ordered the Uber to pick us up?' She nods and we all head out the front to wait. I can see a van parked up the street with someone sitting in the front seat smoking. The glow of the cigarette tip illuminates their face as they take a drag. After a few minutes, they must be finished; they flick their butt out the window. Seriously? I shake my head. The Uber arrives and we all pile in. The two girls I was talking to sit on either side of me, both of them sort of snuggling into me. I don't protest. The ride home only takes a few minutes and we all pile back out and head inside. The two boys break off quickly and disappear with the girls to their rooms, leaving me with the two remaining girls.

'So where is your room, Jacob?' Jen asks.

'It's down the back of the house. I can show you both if you like?'

They look at each other and smile. 'Sure, lead the way.'

I turn and walk through to my room and open the door for them to enter, Jen and Chloe follow walking in. They both walk around in my room looking at my things, I guess judging who I'm. It's very minimalist so they won't get much from me. Some fake photos of my fake family, some normal college student type things, nothing really exciting at all.

We all sit on my bed for a while talking and laughing. Well, the girls are doing most of the talking. I enjoy listening to them, talking about their lives, their families. It relaxes me, letting me feel normal, even if it is only for a little while. I see one of the girl's yawn and take that as my cue to bail.

'Well, I think it is time to go to bed. You two can have my room and I'll crash out on the couch. Do you need anything before I leave you?'

They look at each other. 'Thanks Jacob, that is very nice of you,' Jen smiles at me. 'But you don't need to sleep on the couch if you don't want to. I am sure we could all fit in here nicely.' She looks at the bed and back at me.

I don't take the offer though. I smile, 'No, the couch is good for me,' and head out of the room, closing the door behind me to give them some privacy as I do.

I can hear them giggling as I walk down the hallway. I wonder what they are talking about. I shrug off the thought and grab a blanket from the cupboard and some of the pillows from the other couch before getting myself comfortable. What a weird night. I'm glad it's coming to an end. I really don't know how much longer I can keep up this act for. It's time to get back to work, to my real world. Back to being Shadow.

There has to be someone I could be hunting, making pay for whatever horrible thing they have done. Maybe I could do some research, find my answers about her. My mystery girl.

CHAPTER 18

SLIP THE TAIL

I have been playing nice for weeks now. It's time for me to get back to work, lose this life and move on. I have seen the teams that watch me do changeovers and I think I'm starting to figure out the pattern. A car will do a drive by first. A few minutes later, they will circle back and park behind the van. A few moments go by and then I see the team in the van come out. They chat for a few moments and then swap vehicles.

If I can make my move at the exact time they do handover, I'll have a few minutes while they are distracted to do my thing. I'm going to need Sarina's help to get out of this. I need a plan.

I'm going to use my phone to contact Sarina. I'll have less than thirty seconds to verify my identity and confirm my requests. I hope that will be long enough. I have a hidden code on my phone that will allow me to destroy the evidence on the phone as soon as I'm done, so it won't be any benefit to them in tracking me or finding out who I call.

I have about 15 minutes until handover. I need to get ready. I can see the van parked up the street using the cameras mounted on the guttering of the house. My room is dark and the curtains are pulled across so my watchers are prevented from spotting me at my computer as I keep an eye on them. I walk over to my alarm clock. I hold down the minutes, hours and tune buttons for thirty seconds. I see the time on the clock face blink three times. I have activated the jammer. Only my VPN communication will work now. I have two minutes until the clock is burned out to hide the evidence. I pick up the phone and initiate the hidden app via Siri. I hope this works or I'll be signing my own arrest warrant.

'Siri, execute Shadow Sequence.' The application loads up and connects me to Sarina.

'It's good to finally hear from you Sir. What do you need?'

'Sarina, it's good to talk to you too. I need a way out of here and I need surveillance of the watchers so I can make a clean getaway. Can you provide all that?'

'Affirmative. Sir, you have a ride waiting around the back. I have sent one of the cars to retrieve you. Walk out the front door in exactly 23 seconds. The guards will be doing the changeover. I'm using the car's systems to take over the surveillance signal and will replicate my own in ten seconds. Get ready to move.'

I pause at the front door, waiting for the signal. It's a shame I need to bail on this life. I was starting to like my roommates, even if they are oddballs. No time to reminisce though. Time to get free of my cage.

The street light in front of the house goes out. 'Go now, head left as soon as you hit the footpath and continue to the end of the block. Go fast. Stick to the shadows.'

I go, doing exactly as she said. I get to the footpath and run down the street sticking to the shadows as best I can. 'Drop the phone. Your ride will be in front of you in 15 seconds.'

I drop the phone. As I do, I hear the phone make a weird shriek noise and start to smoke. As I look up, I see a car pull up in front of me. I open the door and jump in. As soon as my door closes, the car takes off again.

'What is our status Sarina, are we in the clear, or do we have company?' I pull my seatbelt on and look behind me.

'We are in the clear, Sir. It will likely be a couple of hours before they notice you are gone. Surveillance has been restored to the original stream and a secondary vehicle has been pulled back from the area. It will likely connect with us shortly. Would you like to go to the safe house on the sunshine coast?'

I take a deep breath. I'm much calmer now I know we have gotten away clean. I just need to keep it that way now. I see a car come up behind us very fast and then settle in at a two-car distance behind. 'Is that our secondary vehicle, Sarina?' I look in the mirror, I can't see anything but lights.

'Yes, Sir. I have activated the safe house and the systems are all coming online. We will be there in under an hour.'

'Make sure we are not followed. Use all means to ensure we are clean before arrival at the safe house.' The secondary car breaks off. 'Where is Tesla two going?' The car's lights turn off as it does, we are running in the dark.

'Going into dark mode, Sir. Tesla two is the honeypot in case we are being followed. Get some rest. I'll wake you when we are getting closer.' That is probably a great idea. I don't know if I'll be able to do it, but I should at least try.

I don't get much sleep. I'm too hyped up from losing my watchers. It is not over yet. They will be looking for me by now or soon at the very least.

We get to the safe house. It's a modern, trendy house, one I sublet out on Stayz, not for the money, but so no one will take any notice when someone strange is arriving and staying there. It is only ever for upmarket guests, so it is rarely rowdy and doesn't get damaged. It has a stunning ocean view, pool and spa area, and is completely secure with high-tech security platforms. Perfect for those more privacy concerned celebrities or an outside of the law hacker.

The house has a hidden room under the pool that none of the guests know about. My tech is all there, ready for me to work at any time. Sarina keeps it all in pristine condition and up to date with my latest tools. The gate opens and we drive in. The lights start to come on inside and the complex is secured.

'Sarina, are we all clear?' The car stays on for a few moments and then powers off.

'Everything is clear, moving to house communications. Do you want your console activated and ready to work?' I get out of the car and head to the door. It opens as I reach it and closes as I walk through.

'Yes, get my workstation ready. I'm going to have a shower first before getting to work. Monitor the situation and alert me of any changes.'

CHAPTER 19

CLEANING MY TRACKS

It's been almost a week since I abandoned my life as Jacob Loxley and slipped my tail. They have been looking for me but I have managed to stay one step ahead. I have been getting ready to make my next move. I have all the access I need to erase everything anyone has on me, fingerprints, photos; everything will be gone. The only thing I can't erase is peoples' memory of me. Humans are the chink in my armour, they will always be the weakness in my cover identities. Memories of me will fade with time, I tried to ensure I was just a passing blip in peoples' lives.

One day that might be an option, wiping peoples' brains that is, you know when they have those bio links in our brains that Elon Musk has been working on, when a hacker and his machine will be one. When I hack you, I'll have access to your brain and its memories as well. I love the idea of being able to download abilities and skills as Neo did in the matrix, I love that movie.

How cool would it be though to be able to download skills and abilities? School would not be necessary. We would just download the ability, the knowledge we need and that would be it. Although by the time that comes about, we will all have robots doing everything for us and none of us will work anymore, not really. I don't know if that is a scenario I would like to live in or not. Yes, there would be some benefits, but I feel we would lose ourselves a little.

I'm getting off track though. I need to start the countdown. I grab my coffee and head out to the back deck. It is beautiful out here. I never really stop to look at it or just enjoy it. The landscape designer did a brilliant job out here. I can see why all the Stayz guests give it a five-star rating. It really is something. Enough distraction, I need to get to work.

'Sarina, open the access to the bunker please.' The deck between myself and the pool starts to pull apart and stairs lead down to a door underneath the base of the pool. I walk down the stairs. As I get closer to the door a bio scanner analyses me. I stop in front of the door and wait for the verification to complete. After a few moments, the door light goes green and it opens. As I step inside, the upper deck starts to close back together and the entry door moves back into the closed position.

'Sarina, what is the status? Do we know who the girl is yet? I want to know if she is going to be a problem for us. Is she a threat I need to prepare for? Are we in a position to start the eraser protocols?' I walk over and sit on my chair. It is strange to think I have over fifty thousand litres of water above my head. Cooling for my systems is never a problem down here. It's always a nice constant cool temperature, that is for sure.

'Yes, we are ready to initiate Eraser Protocols Sir. On the matter of the girl, no further progress. She has no digital footprint, much like yourself.'

I swing around in my chair, looking towards my main screen.

'Initiate Eraser Protocols.' I take a sip of my coffee and I can see my programs at work. They are deleting my information, photos, DNA samples, and anything else that can be found of me anywhere. Social media, police or transport systems, everywhere.

I replace photos with images of someone who was generated by Sarina. They're not a real person, just derived from facial similarities to me but different enough so they wouldn't suspect me of being the same person. For anyone who has seen me, they could believe their memory is just a little faded and that must be the right person. Not everyone will be fooled but they won't have any images left of me, so it will be hard to compare.

'Process now completed, Sir. Do you want to destroy the Loxley bunker?'

I consider for a moment, is destroying the bunker necessary or is it just overkill? If I action my plan, I could be giving them more evidence to catch me with, but it could mean I could learn more about my mystery girl. Is she worth the potential risk? Do I stick my head up and see what happens? I could give them a clue to look at and see if it brings me any information on who exactly I am dealing with. I don't even know if she will come to the scene but it's worth the risk. The explosion will destroy the whole site. Nothing but fragments will survive. It will give me a look at my watchers though, find out who is really after me.

'Destroy the Loxley Bunker but leave the cameras online. I want to see who shows up.'

I see a massive explosion, rubble flying everywhere, the camera's shake and there is dust and smoke everywhere. I bet that woke up the neighbours, even if they are two kilometres away.

Now I wait…

CHAPTER 20

WATCHING THE HUNTERS

It is less than twenty minutes before I see the flashing of red and blue lights near the bunker. There are at least twenty vehicles, a mix of police, fire, ambulance and what looks like it could be the bomb squad. They move in first, scanning the area for threats, while the police surround the area making sure no one gets in or out. They are being very cautious which is smart. I'm sure they have no idea of what this is, or who they are dealing with. I watch them fluff about for a few hours with scanners and drones near the crater. The sun is starting to come up. I think it's time for some breakfast. I get up and walk to the bunker door.

'Sarina, is the coast clear to exit?' I wait while the perimeter is checked.

'The area is clear, it is safe to proceed.'

I open the door and the deck above me opens for me to exit. I make my way up and head towards the kitchen. I feel like a bacon and egg roll. That, with a cup of coffee, should get all my neurons firing properly. I need to be alert when they arrive.

'Sarina, notify me if anything changes or if the team we have been looking for arrives.'

I start to cook my breakfast, busying myself so I don't keep thinking about her. It only takes a few minutes before it's ready and I'm sitting down looking out over the backyard. I should give the pool a go. What is the point of having a heated mineral pool that will ease your body's aches and pains if I don't even give it a try?

This roll is just what I needed. I'm starting to feel much better already. Nice and alert. It is like that 2:30 pm urge to snooze on a long day in the office, if you have a snack, you are good to go for another few hours at least. Not that I have ever done a 9-5 job, but I'm guessing that is what it's like.

'Sorry to interrupt, Sir, but a convoy of black SUV's has just arrived. This could be them.' I jump to my feet. I guess this is breakfast to go now. I grab my breakfast and head for the bunker. As I approach, it opens for me to walk straight down the stairs, the scan is completed and the door unlocks.

I head over to the main screen. 'Show me.'

I see three SUVs at the gate with the police, talking to the driver it would seem. The officer calls someone over the radio and a few seconds later the convoy is waved through. Okay, let us see who you all are. 'Sarina, I want images of all occupants of these vehicles. Run them through every database. Agencies, crime groups, find out who they are.'

As I see them all get out of the vehicles, most of the occupants head off to position themselves in defensive positions. They are the soldiers. I wonder if any of them gave me the bruises on my ribs. They are still green and yellow after weeks have passed. Then I see her.

I almost feel my heart miss a beat. It's definitely her.

I watch them head over to the crater. She is just looking over the scene, surveying what is in front of her. It would appear the others are waiting for her direction, is she in charge? She seems to notice them watching, she says something to them and they disperse, getting to work. I wish I had audio on these cameras. I would like to hear her voice.

I watch them work for hours. They are like little worker ants scurrying around collecting everything. I can see by what they are collecting they won't have much to go on. Nothing is intact; nothing will be usable. I erased it all before I detonated the bunker, so even if by some miracle one of the drives survive and they can recover data they would still need to break my encryption. I don't even know if I could do that, not in the short term at least.

I see the sun start to set and the team is packing up. I'm guessing they have everything they think could be useful. It's all loaded up in a secured storage box and put into the back of one of the SUVs. I see her looking around.

She stops and looks directly at the camera I'm watching them from.

She calls over one of the team and says something to them. They both look in the direction of the camera. Oh crap, the game is up, they know I'm watching them. Two of the team members start walking towards the camera. I know I have to burn out the cameras but I don't want to stop watching her.

'Sarina, burn out all cameras at the Loxley bunker.' I watch her for a few more moments before the process is completed and the cameras are burned out.

There literally would have been a puff of smoke come out of each camera, if they were close enough to see it. I need to find her, to know who she is. 'Sarina, initiate the search for the girl with the new images. Find her team, who they all are and every detail about her you can find. If you have any trouble inform me so I can assist.' I hear the servers kick into high gear. Sarina is using all the available resources, not just here I assume across all of my bunkers, there is a few of them and she is part of all of them.

CHAPTER 21

HUNTING THE HUNTERS

I have been hunting down my hunters one by one with the images I captured from the bunker I blew to pieces. Sarina searched every database and every last corner of the internet with my facial recognition platform. They all work for the Australian Signals Directorate it would seem but that is just a guess, none of them has any official records that would specifically indicate they work for ASD but all have similar backgrounds in military or Australian Security Intelligence Organisation or something like that. I have had Sarina scouring the internet and federal databases for them. It's a similar story when I find each of them. They all have a paper trail until a few years ago, some more or less and then nothing. Not a single thing at all. Like they vanished off the face of the earth.

Not very smooth really. They should've given them identities, had them continue in normal jobs. Tech support, cleaners, managers, it doesn't matter what it is as long as it makes sense. Don't give a General a cleaner's job, that will raise flags. You could easily put them with a consultancy firm as a security consultant or risk advisers. That would look like a convincing transition from military or government over to the private sector. Even I could buy that, if they sold it right. Government agencies don't tend to do that though for anyone who isn't a field operative. Maybe it's too much work or they are just lazy, I don't know. They just let them ghost, which is more obvious, if you ask me.

Most of the people I have identified are the muscle, the ones who broke off to secure the site, the other four doing the digging around my tech gear are not coming up so easy. I'm guessing all of them are analysts, like in cyber, digital forensics, or some sort of technical roles. I know I'm stereotyping here, but they just look like techie people, not your revenge of the nerds type people but the ones you would see at a cybersecurity conference or capture the flag time hacking events. Think one of those big gaming events for hackers where they all go hang out and talk shop.

Except for the girl. A little spunky, intelligent, and beautiful. I need to focus. She is my enemy here, my opponent. After the bunker, I know she is in charge of the team. She is the one pulling their strings, she might not be the top of the string, but she is definitely who I need to focus on. I need to remember that.

I have been doing some searching myself on top of Sarina's efforts, not because I don't think she can't find them. It's a weird need of mine to look for her. I can't help it. I just need to do it. It is just this niggling itch I need to keep scratching or it flares up in an uncontrollable need. I have never had this type of infatuation about a girl before. Correction, about *anyone* before. The only thing that even comes close was my drive to get revenge for my parents. This is different though. It's like I'm infatuated with her, like I'm being drawn to her.

I need to get a grip.

Yes, I need to find her, but I'm only doing it so I know my enemy, the one I need to defeat. Nothing more.

I have been at it for days now. I'm coming up with nothing. She is more of a ghost than I am. I didn't think that was possible. Out of pure luck, I stumble across a news article, something about a school winning a hacking competition a few months ago. I almost dismiss it, but something pulls me back. The contestant wiped the floor with the other competitors. I don't mean just beat them. I mean blew them all out of the water. Like what they asked her to do was just like playing with toddlers. It was as though she defeated them with just her muscle memory.

They took out a bonus round set up by the hosts of the event, to win their school all this new computer equipment funded by the government as part of the prize pool. I bet all that new free equipment made her school happy. The competitor was a girl, a year twelve student. Could this be her? I hunt for more details, scouring the web to find a video or photo. There has to be something here. Someone had to have gotten a photo of her.

I find a promo shot of the winner accepting the award for the competition on their school's website. It's a little blurry, but it could be her. 'Sarina, analyse and reprocess this image, I need a clear shot of the winner.' It takes only a few moments before the image reappears on the screen with a crisp and clear shot of the winner.

It is her. Maybe six months ago or more, but it is her. The one I have been looking for. Samantha. Her name is Samantha. I start to dig deeper into her life, her father, her estranged mother. I look at her school grades. She is an above-average student but I think this is all a lie for the world to see, like Jacob was for me. I wonder who her real self is? With someone of her skills, this is not her first rodeo. She must have left a trail, one that brought the feds looking her way.

I dig through the dark web looking for anything that could help me see her work, that could match her skills. I find nothing but whispers, secrets being passed from hacker to hacker. Then I see it. A message for me, almost calling me out. This was when I was in custody. The timing of it couldn't be a coincidence. She was testing me, to see if I was sitting in that interrogation room. I didn't respond, which probably was enough to confirm in her mind I was Shadow. The guts to call out the devil, the shadow of the dark web, not many would have the courage to come at me like that. If she was wrong, she could have unleashed hell on herself with that move. She didn't seem to fear that.

Foresight.

That is her true self, her hacker self. I need to find out everything I can about her. I redirect Sarina to search for whispers of her hacker identity, Foresight and I'll look at her worldly identity. I'll know everything about her.

CHAPTER 22

FIRST CONTACT

The more I dig into Foresight the more I'm in awe of her skills, she has done some things I can only dream of, she is honourable and does not do what she does for financial gain or revenge or anything like that. She does it because it is right. She is the one from whom I stole the system burnout attack. She took on the cartel and lives to talk about it. She is ballsy and lethal. If I'm honest, I think she scares me a little. I have never been scared to come up against anyone, ever, until now.

She is righteous and does whatever it takes to succeed. I think I found my future wife, if she doesn't wipe the floor with me and lock me up for the rest of my life. Wow, that's a conundrum. I want to know her. I'm scared of coming up in a true battle against her as I know I could lose. That's never a thought I have considered before, losing to anyone in the cyber world. My match, if what I feel is true, which it is as it seems.

What do I do? Do I run, turn into the shadow as I have done before or do I stay and risk it all, for a girl I don't even really know? Yes, I know her achievements and honestly, they are probably enough on their own, but I have never even talked to her. I need to get a grip. Don't put everything on the line for someone you have never even spoken to, never even chatted online. Look, that would be a start, we're hackers, that's our real world, not the physical space of flesh and blood.

That's what I need to do. I need to reach out to her, talk to her, introduce myself. It would mean a game of skill, as I know she would do her job, she would hunt me. I'm her target. The enemy, but just maybe I could change her opinion of me. Show her we are the same, just different circumstances, that moulded our life paths. We could be on the same side or at least not be enemies. Is it worth the risk? I need to think about this. If she wins and I'm caught, it would mean jail. A lot of jail for me, I would say. Can I live with that decision?

This could be my chance to have what my parents had, that real love, one with no bonds, one that can grow stronger with each day. Could I have what they once had before it was ripped away? Is that even still a possibility for me? It has to be. I need to at least try, for my mum and dad. They would have wanted me to risk everything for a chance at true love.

I take a nice slow deep breath. Let's just take the first step. I'll wait for her to come online. I have her slack handle. I watch, waiting for what seems like hours. It's green, she's online. Calm now, let's play it cool. Let's just have some fun and see where it goes.

What do I say?

'I hear you are looking for me.' I wait, eager to see if she will play along. I start to type a response to her inevitable question. She will ask me who I am, to verify I'm Shadow, but I need to wait for her.

'Who are you?' she asks, as predicted. I smile and hit enter to send my already typed response.

'Shadow. You already know that though, don't you, Foresight?' That should get her thinking.

'Yes, I do.'

I shoot back another quick response. 'So what set your sights on me? Whose toes did I step on to ruffle your feathers? Or do you just want to prove you are the best in the schoolyard? You have done some cool things. I'm impressed, a perfect girl.'

Mmmm was that a bit much? Keep cool. I don't want to come on too strong. Just be cool. She is taking her time to respond, she must be considering what I'm after, what I know. That's what I would be doing.

'I'll take that as a compliment,' she responds. I wait, giving her time to take the lead, to let her do her thing. 'You take what isn't yours. I don't like that. You might target scum bags but you do it for profit, not for good.'

Ouch. She is not impressed with what I do for money but it's not all bad, she mentioned I only target scumbags. It's something. I guess I'll have to work with that.

I need to be careful. A bad response here could mean I get shut out, put in the enemy category with no return. Think, come on, what is my move?

'It's true, I make money from the scum of the earth. It is expensive staying invisible and the money I take was never really theirs in the first instance. We don't all work for government agencies do we, Sam?'

That might have been a step too far.

'Why don't you just turn yourself in and save me the headache of finding you? Trust me on this though, I will find you.' She wants to play, does she? Okay, let's play.

'I was hoping you would say that. I love games. None before you have tested me as much. This is going to be fun, may the best hacker win…' I'll leave that to sit for a while, it's game on.

CHAPTER 23

THE GAME STARTS

I get to work right away. I look for everything I can, any accounts she has that I could use against her. I look for anything at her house that could be used to my advantage. I need her to know just who she's up against, what I can do, without scaring her. What should I do first? I'm going to do some orders. Why not have some fun? Everyone could do with toilet paper, right? Two pallet loads of toilet paper should do. You never want to run out. Her father is going to love that. Oooh, I'm good. Now what? I don't want to steal from her, so the bank accounts are off-limits.

How about I wake them up nice and early? Maybe have breakfast waiting. What would I like for breakfast if someone was going to order it and have it delivered? It needs to be good, something she would enjoy. We are hackers; this is our first dance, our first real interaction, a duel of sorts... almost a date... I brush the thought aside and decide on a nice English breakfast. Sam's father, John, seems like he would enjoy a hearty breakfast. It will be on Sam, of course, but that doesn't mean the meal shouldn't be thoughtful. I tell the delivery person the sender is a Mr Shadow. Perfect. How early is too early? 5 am should be perfect. Early enough to be dramatic but not too early as to make Sam hate me for it either.

Now for the alarm clock. I get to work putting together a selection of high octane power songs, something that will get their blood pumping. I take control of her smart speaker in the lounge room. Sam, it was a mistake leaving it open to the internet, you are making this game a little too easy for me. I turn the volume to maximum and set it to start at 5 am tomorrow. This is going to really piss her off, especially the two pallets of toilet paper.

How should I soften the blow? Maybe some flowers, on me, so it is a true gift. The card, what do I put on the card? I got it.

'I never got your number at the station, Sam. Now I have it. I have all your contacts. I hope you like the flowers. I thought it would be rude of me to not give flowers on a first date. This is kinda like a hacker's version of a first date, so here you are.' How to finish it off? 'I hope you are enjoying our game. It's your move.'

I hope she likes the flowers.

I should probably do a transaction in her bank accounts, something small, just so she knows I have access. A $1 transaction to a charity should do it. Now a description so she knows it was me.

'Just so you know I could have. I'll not take what isn't mine.' That should be enough for my first move of our game of hackers' chess.

Perfect. The game is afoot. I wish I could see their reaction. I don't have any way of getting eyes in that house, the smart speaker doesn't have a camera. I'll just have to imagine it and just wait for her response. I better get some sleep. She will fight back. I'll need to be prepared. I set my alarm for 5 am and curl up in bed. I struggle to go to sleep with the excitement of what I know will come tomorrow.

What will she do in retaliation? Will she play the game or will she leave me hanging? I wonder if she will like the flowers. Oh, I'm not getting any sleep tonight, all I can think about is her and this game of ours. I have never felt so alive.

CHAPTER 24

RETALIATION

I barely slept last night. I couldn't get her out of my mind. I relocated to a motel about an hour's drive from the safe house. I may need to escape quickly and would like a place to be able to get to and go to ground if needed. I know Foresight is quite skilled at what she does and I have basically kicked the hornet's nest, so to speak. Maybe not the smartest thing I have done but I did try to soften the blow with some flowers. That won't be enough to slow down the wrath that is surely coming my way. It's coming and I don't want to put all my cards out on the table straight up. I could lose and I need to be prepared for that.

That in itself, is a new feeling for me: *I could lose.* It is crazy that I may have found my match in skill. No that's not true. If I'm really honest with myself, I think she could be my superior when it comes to natural skill. I may be a little more resourceful and potentially a little more prepared for this duel of ours, but if it comes down to just skill, I know I'll lose. That scares me but at the same time is the most exhilarating feeling. To make it even worse, I think she is one of the most beautiful people I have ever seen.

There is just something about her. She is naturally beautiful, yes, but there is a fire in her eyes, this electricity I can't resist losing myself in. I know I should resist this crush I have on her. I should just drop this game of hacker skills and get out of here while I still can. I know she is trying to catch me to arrest me over the business with the politician, but I'm hoping deep down I can change that. Get her to see me as more than just a target. Maybe as a friend, maybe more.

Oh, I need to snap out of this. I'm getting distracted again. I have it bad. I need to take the emotion out of the equation. This could cost me my freedom if I get it wrong and Foresight wipes the floor with me. I close my eyes and clear my head of anything that isn't related specifically to our hacker's duel. *Get your head in the game Shadow. It's game time, the onslaught is coming.*

It's been about thirty minutes since the deliveries were made. Nothing, no response. I can feel her hunting me. I don't know how I know but I can just feel it in my core, call it my Spidey sense or something. She has probably secured what I broke and now it is my turn to be hunted. What will she do? How is she going to find me? Have I made a mistake that will lead her to me? I have ensured nothing I did could be traced to me, not the deliveries, not the flowers, not the bank transactions. With an opponent like Foresight, I can't be complacent. I can't leave any crumbs that could reveal anything, she will use it against me; that is something I can be certain of.

I recheck my actions. I don't want to make it too easy on her, so I better ensure I haven't left a trace. I get about halfway through and then I see it. The power is dropping out for miles around me. As I look out the window, I can see the whole neighbourhood go into darkness. The sun hasn't risen from its slumber yet, so the darkness envelops everything. I don't think it's a coincidence. I think it could be Foresight's work. Well done, well done, indeed. I have to admit I'm impressed. To have that sort of widespread effect on a large utility like power takes some skill. Foresight is taking a bit of a risk. This kind of tactic wouldn't be an ASD approved move. This is very ballsy indeed.

I flick over to my secondary internet connection and fire up slack.

'Nicely played, Sam. Nicely played.' That really was a great move, one that definitely caught me by surprise. I need to be on my A game. Focus. 'Did you like your flowers? I hope it wasn't too girly for you being pink and all.'

I sit now just watching the screen. She is keeping me hanging. Suddenly I see the app spring to life.

'Yes, thank you, but it turns out I probably paid for them. So, I should be thanking myself.'

Oh wow, she thinks I'm so cheap I would send her flowers for our first hacker's date, with her own money? No way, I have to set that straight.

'No, actually, I paid. The flowers were all me. The toilet paper though, that's all you ☺' I bet she thinks she has me now, that she can trace the payment information. I made sure that wasn't possible, but I'll give her a few seconds to start looking. I let about a minute go by before messaging, 'No point checking the transaction info. It is not mine and it won't lead you back to me.'

A couple of minutes go by with nothing. She is about to make her next move; I can sense it. What is it going to be? My heart races; I'm loving this. Suddenly I'm offline, she has disabled my internet service. That was fast and a clever move. Oh crap, if she has my connection, she is probably tracing my location as we speak. It's time to move. Just one more message. One won't hurt. It takes me a few minutes to crack the motel WiFi and get back online. Not much of a challenge, but not much is these days.

I reopen slack and send another message.

'Nice move, Sam. You should probably turn the power back on

though. I'm moving on now anyway.' I pack up my gear and hit the road. I can use the blackout to slip away unseen. I know she will be looking for me, so why not have a little bit of fun? I maneuverer just out of sight of a known camera and pop my head out so the camera can see me. I smile and wave at the camera. I slip back into the shadows and make my escape. I think Foresight will appreciate my wave. It's rude not to say goodbye after all.

CHAPTER 25

EXIT STRATEGY

I pick up my phone. I need to find the best way out of here before Foresight finds me. She will, if I'm not careful. I unlock the phone and connect to Sarina.

'I need a vehicle, Sarina. What do you have close by?'

A few moments go by before she responds, 'I have taken control of a Porsche Cayman, take your next left and two blocks down you will find it open and running by the time you get to it but be fast, the owners might be home.' I pick up my pace. Following Sarina's directions, I take the next left, always keeping to the shadows to avoid any cameras that may be around. I haven't scoped this space out before so I'm running blind.

I get to the home and see the car running in the driveway with the garage open, ready for me to take. I pause for a moment to get a feel for the situation. It all looks good to me so I make my move. It only takes a few moments for me to be in the car and reversing out of the driveway. As I touch the road at the end of the driveway, I see the garage door start to close and an automatic gate close in front of me.

'Good work, Sarina.'

Now where? I don't want to go back to the safe house, not yet anyway. I need to ensure I'm clean and Foresight doesn't know where I am.

Sarina's voice comes over the car internal speakers. She must have full access to the vehicle in-car computer systems.

'Sir, we need to head north and fast. The local camera network is being scanned for your location as we speak. We need to get as much distance as possible before this car is identified and we need to abandon it. I have already initiated Shadow1 to meet you at Noosa, close to the secondary bunker. We will do a hot-swap if needed. Your ETA is forty minutes so you need to get moving.'

I smile, I'll get to see how well this Porsche moves. I accelerate dramatically, feeling the car change attitude almost instantly from this nice and friendly luxury cruiser to some sort of wild beast. It screams at my request, lurching forward with purpose. This is going to be fun. I push the car to its limits, but it seems to take it in its stride. I might have to add one of these to my fleet. I'm making good progress, but this kind of driving is going to bring attention. I just need to get to Shadow1 before Foresight gets to me.

'Sir, we have been located. The vehicle tracking systems have been accessed and local cameras are scanning for this vehicle. You need to rendezvous with Shadow1 as soon as possible. ETA is looking like fifteen minutes at current speeds.' Sam is closing in on me. She really is something. I shake off the distraction and push forward with more purpose.

A few more minutes go by with the outside world flying by almost in a blur. I'm going way too fast but I don't have any time to waste. I can feel her getting closer.

'Sir we have a problem. Two vehicles are closing in on you from different directions. They are going to try and box you in. Prepare for a hot-swap before going dark. Take the next left and exit the car at the end of the street. Shadow1 is on the other side of the path going between the two buildings. You will need to run as fast as you can, they will be right on your tail.' I take a deep breath and speed towards the end of the street. 'Stop now, it is on your left.'

I screech to a stop, swing open the door, grabbing my bag as I do and exit the vehicle. I leave it still running with the door open as I run down the path. I see Shadow1 pull up and I pick up my pace. The sweat is beading on my forehead as I run with everything I have. I reach the car. I can hear a commotion on the street behind me.

They have arrived.

Shadow1 goes dark, all lights go out and I dive in the back seat and just say, 'Go!' The car surges to life, heading to I don't know where, but I stay quiet, no sound, nothing to track me by, nothing to give me away. We're heading back south and continue this way for thirty minutes or more, maybe Sarina is taking me back to the safe house, not the bunker.

Eventually, the lights on the car turn on. 'Sir, we have avoided capture and have made a clean getaway. We are returning to the safe house. There is no need to go to ground at this time but I'll monitor our situation and adapt if needed.'

I relax a little. It was a close one. If they had caught me there would be no escaping this time. They would certainly not believe me that I wasn't Shadow anymore. Jail would be my new home for a long, long time.

The rest of the trip goes by without any further events, just a nice relaxing drive back down the coast. When we arrive at the safe house, Sarina scans the area before continuing to enter the property. For today at least, it's over. I think I have to resign myself; I'm losing this hackers' duel. Foresight is it seems the superior but I still have some fight left in me. It's not over yet. I think I need to be careful about my next move though or I'll get myself some very uncomfortable new bracelets and a free permanent motel room at the local government dark dingy hole they throw people like me in. The thought gives me chills.

CHAPTER 26

WATCHING

It's been over a week since I went underground, the close call with the strike team. They really did come close to getting me. If I didn't have Sarina's help, I would have been stuck in a deep, dark hole, rotting for who knows how long. Just the thought of it still gives me shivers. I haven't ventured out since that night. I think it's best I keep a low profile while she is looking for me. I know she won't give up her hunt because I've been messaging her most of the week. It is crazy, I know, but I can't help it. I need to talk to her, like it's some sort of drug withdrawal that keeps eating at me until I scratch the itch. I have dropped the game and have just been talking to her about our misadventures, nothing detailed enough for her to use against me or anything, just talking shop.

She has been very open when talking with me. I don't know if it is an act and she is just trying to make me feel safe. Allow me to get comfortable so I make a mistake and give up some sort of information she can use against me. I feel like something more is happening though, a connection, a friendship or something. Not something either of us expected or, in Foresight's case, can allow to occur. I get it. Her job is to catch me and she is either going to have to fail or I'm going to have to lose. If I'm honest, neither option appeals to me. I don't want her to fail, to look bad for not catching her target, even if that target is me. I don't want to go to jail either though, so it's a tough spot we're in.

I have been watching her, everything she has been doing. It feels a bit stalkerish, if I'm honest, and I think I need to stop. I have been telling myself it is to ensure I know where she is and if they are about to find me, for my protection. I honestly think it's just because I'm infatuated with her and I like to see her. This is the only way I can. I believe she knows I'm watching, but she is not 100% sure if she is just being paranoid or not. She isn't, but I'm not going to admit to her I'm probably crossing some boundaries.

I can see her getting ready to take her mustang for a drive. It's the only flashy thing she owns. A little out of what I expected, but it suits her. From what I can see, she didn't pay for it but it turned up in her name just after that hacking competition she blitzed. It must have been a bonus gift, not a bad bonus, if you ask me. I will have to ask her about it sometime.

It seems to be her way of shaking off the stresses of life and clearing her mind. I see the fascination, pushing the car to the edge, the roar of the engine, the feel of it struggling to hold on. It's an exhilarating feeling and one I enjoy myself. She has been driving around for almost half an hour.

I have been tracking her but I'm not the only one. I sensed it a few minutes after she left her house. The same camera systems I was utilising had another foreign presence and after a few more minutes I saw a white van following her at a distance, probably because it couldn't keep up a fast a pace as Sam.

Something's going to happen, I don't know what but I know it's coming.

Sam is in danger.

I have to find a way to warn her or stop it from happening. There has to be something I could do, but I feel frozen in my computer chair, eyes glued to the screens.

A second vehicle jumps through an intersection, taking out Sam's car.

They hit it so hard it causes the mustang to spin, clipping the gutter. The car flips over several times before coming to rest on its roof.

Sam isn't moving.

I can't see much from the street camera across the road from where her car came to a stop. Wait, I can see her fidgeting, figuring out what has happened. A guy jumps out of the car that hit her and rushes towards her. He drops down and pulls her out of the car. He doesn't stop there though, he scoops her up and as he does that white van arrives. He climbs through the open side door and disappears with Sam. Holly crap, she has been taken, but by who and why?

'Sarina, track that van. Do not let it slip away. Forget stealth, make as much noise as you need, but just don't lose her. I can't lose her.' Sarina gets to work while I gather intel from the video feeds on who has grabbed her. I start facial recognition searches on the guy who pulled her out of the car. It only takes a few moments before I get a match. Oh crap, this is retaliation for her last big hit as a hacker outside of the ASD. The guy is one of those human traffickers from the cartel. She literally burned down their operation, how did they find her? Someone must have talked, given her up; there was no evidence. I'll put a pin in the problem of who gave her up, I'll revisit that one later.

'Sir, the van has stopped at a warehouse on Brisbane's northside. I am sending the location to your screen now.' I take a look at the site and search for any digital footprint, anything I can use to see what is happening. There is a web-facing camera system with default login details. People make it too easy for me sometimes. I log in and search the cameras. Found her.

She is tied to a chair in a dingy room with a guy standing opposite her. He seems to be talking to her. There is no audio but I can see his mouth move. I move the camera around to get a better look at the rest of room. What I see makes my stomach lurch.

An array of what looks like torture tools have been arranged on a nearby table. I don't think I can handle seeing them do that stuff to Sam, I have to find a way to stop it.

I pan the camera back to look at her. She sees the movement and stares into the camera. I wonder what she is thinking. Does she know it's me? Or does she think it is one of her sick captors, watching the show. The man picks up one of the knives and walks over to Sam. He places the blade on her skin and makes a small, precise cut. I can see Sam is fighting back her screams. She is in pain and I can't take it. I snatch up a waste paper basket sitting beside my desk and heave into it. Wiping my mouth with the back of my wrist, I call out to Sarina.

'It's time to call in a favour I'm owed. Reach out to Deano, it's time his team got to work.'

CHAPTER 27

ON ROUTE

I was intending to call this favour for myself one day, when I had no other option but I can't let this happen to Sam, I just can't. Sarina has put out the call to Deano and his team. I just have to wait now until I hear back from them. I hope they are close. I need this to be handled quickly.

I met Deano and his crew a few years ago, one of their team had been captured during a job and they needed help infiltrating an organisation to find where they had been taken. I had heard of the team's skills. They are the best at getting a job done in situations most people would never dream of even attempting. They're fast, accurate, and deadly.

I knew having them on my side would one day pay off. I'd helped them not for money but an agreement that if ever I needed their help they would come, they would do what they do best. My phone suddenly comes to life. A blocked number is calling. This will probably be him. I lift the phone to my ear, pressing the green button as I do.

'Shadow, my good friend. It's been too long. I assume if you are searching me out you require our help?'

Straight to the point is perfect, I don't have time for pleasantries.

'Yes, I need your help and I need it fast. How quick can you get to Brisbane? I have a friend who is in a bit of a spot. Some people have taken her and she needs to be exfiltrated before it's too late. I don't need it to be quiet. I don't need it clean; I just need her safe.'

I can hear the sense of desperation in my voice. Deano picks up on it too.

'I'm sensing this girl is important to you, Shadow. If she is important to you, then she is important to me. She is our family now, as are you. We are already in Brisbane preparing for another job, but it can wait.' I take a deep breath. They are already here, thank Christ. I look over at the screen and see that man beating Sam, hurting her. It makes my blood boil.

'Thank you, Deano, Thank you. This means a lot to me.' The emotional appeal isn't like me, and a few seconds pass before he responds.

'Send me through your friend's details and anything you have to make our job easier. Do you have eyes inside we can use?'

'Yes, I have access to the camera's inside and a full floor plan of the location. I also believe I know where she is but it's not certain, you may need to improvise.' I turn to the computer and start to gather the details.

'Consider your friend safe. She will be back in your arms in no time.' I smile. I like the sound of that.

'Actually Deano, it is not like that. She's hunting me. She is my opponent in what you could call a hackers' duel. One I'm sad to say I think I was losing.'

'So let me get this right, she is trying to take you down but you want us to save her?'

It's a little strange now that I think about it.

'Yes, she is ASD. She is essentially my opponent and she is hunting me. It's more than that though. There's something about her, something I'm willing to risk everything for. I think I have feelings for her I never thought would be possible for me. I can't explain it, Deano. I know it doesn't make sense, but I can't let anything happen to her, I just can't.'

His response is fast. 'Sounds like you've fallen for this girl, my friend. Forbidden love is a strong thing.' My fingers pause on the keyboard for a moment as he speaks. Do I love Sam? Deano continues, 'I'll save her for you my friend, worry not. Now we mobilise, send me what you have and wait for the boom…'

The phone line goes dead and he is gone. I stop trying to sort through my feelings and send through everything I have. 'Sarina, we will need to run interference for them, we can't have anyone getting in their way, it could cost Sam or one of Deano's team their lives.' I think it's time to go noisy, show them they have messed with the wrong people.

'Sir, Deano's team is thirty minutes out. I'm clearing the way for them so we can cut that time down. I'm monitoring the police channels and will keep them out of our way.'

I get to work taking full control of the network the cameras are on and gathering everything I can to help Deano. This needs to be perfect, with no mistakes. It only takes me a few minutes and I have everything we need. Door access systems, security alarms, and even the perimeter gates. I own their network and we are going to bring down hell upon them. This is going to get real noisy, real fast. These scumbags are not going to know what hit them.

If my count is correct, there are about twenty people at the location, which should be easy work for Deano's team. I send the updated info to the exfiltration team. We are almost ready.

'Sir, the team is arriving at the site. The area is clear of any interference and we are a go…'

CHAPTER 28

RESCUE

Deano and his crew are outside the secured facility where Sam is being held. They are in their van waiting for the green light. I'm watching the guards patrolling the area, they are sticking to a set route. A few more moments and they will pass by where the team are waiting. I watch patiently as they go past and continue to walk to the other side of the facility. 'It's a go Deano, it's a go…'

The team exit the vehicle, covered in black head to toe. I can only see them because of the slight reflection on the night vision gear they are wearing. They approach the gate and enter the credentials I gave them. It opens, and they walk through.

I launch the four drones I've positioned on top of the van. They all have infrared cameras so I can track the team and protect them from oncoming enemies. I added a little something special for the captors, thanks to Deano, that will leave them distracted for the escape. That is if there is any left to distract. Sarina takes control of the drones and positions them to get a 360-degree view of the team and the surrounding area. I'm their eyes in the sky and will be able to help guide them out after they have Sam.

They make their way around to the side of the building closest to where I believe Sam is being held. They are like ghosts, hidden in the night's shadow. As they make their way to the entry point, I see them silently eliminate several guards. No noise, no fuss, just gone, with their heat fading away on the cameras. I see the team position themselves for entry. I hear the three clicks on the radio. That's my cue.

I access the door control systems and a few seconds later I release the door. The red light on the panel turns green. Three more taps on the radio. They are going in. They enter swiftly and aggressively, no longer looking to be quiet. It's time for the BOOM, as Deano likes to say. Guns are firing in all directions. From the drones, I see guards dropping like flies. One after another but the team continues to advance on Sam's location.

It's chaos, explosions, gunfire. I can barely make out who is who on the internal cameras. I don't know how they do it but it's like they are almost invisible. I see guards drop, explosions, but barely a glimpse of the team. I'm glad they are on my side. I can see from the mayhem that they must be getting close to Sam's location.

I look at the camera from her room. The guy has stopped, his body turned toward the direction of the door. He can probably hear the gunfire and is trying to figure out what the hell is going on. I don't think they would have many people who would have the guts or strength to strike them, this would be very unexpected. Sam looks confused, swaying in her seat. I think she is a little out of it. I hope we are in time to prevent her from any permanent damage. She looks in bad shape. I'm angry I could not stop this before it happened, but at least she will be safe soon.

The door suddenly swings open. The team flood the room as one and spread out to cover the whole space. One of them approaches the man. He goes to fire a weapon but I see a blade swipe quickly across his body and he drops to his knees. One of the team looks up at the camera, removes the gun from his holster, and fires several rounds into the torturer's chest. He falls to the floor and I don't see any further movement. The gunman must be Deano. That was likely for me, for what he did to Sam. Swift and lethal revenge. He likely deserved a slow and painful death for what he has done, but that will have to do for now. His bosses can suffer that fate once she is safe.

Two of the team cut the restraints holding Sam to the chair. One of them picks her up and carries her out of the room with the other members flanking them.

'Sarina, get ready for the exit. We need to clear the way.' They only take a few minutes and they come out of the same door they entered earlier. There isn't much resistance left, they have almost annihilated the whole force at the site in minutes. I send the command to release the gates, all of them, all the locks. Everything is open. They make their way across the field to their van. 'Deano, you have guards approaching from both sides, four on your three o'clock and three more at eight o'clock.' I see the team stop and a quick rapid-fire erupts. The guards drop to the ground within seconds and the team picks up their pace to the gate.

'As soon as your team is clear, I'll start eraser protocol, followed by our light show.' A quick three clicks on the radio confirm he has a copy. They go through the gate and enter the van. It starts and heads down the road without any lights. They are still using the night vision to see their way.

I kick off the eraser protocol, clearing all footage from the systems, erasing all systems logs and finally completely corrupting the entire system with a good old cryptovirus. It will take less than a minute to encrypt everything they have. As a bonus, it may reach out over their network to other sites, giving them a bit more of a punch to the stomach. It's done. I look at the drone footage and see the van is now at the end of the street. It's time for the light show.

'Sarina, bring on the BOOM.' All four drones move into position above the designated locations on the facility. Suddenly, they all crash down through glass ceiling panels through windows into each location. They can no longer fly but that doesn't matter for what is about to happen. 'Detonate the charges,' I say. A few moments later, the charges on the drones Deano graciously provided for clean up explode, destroying most of the structure and set the police scanners alive with chatter.

My phone jumps to life. I answer it.

'Shadow, you can sleep easy tonight my friend, your girl is safe. If you ever need us again, we will be at your call. We are forever family.' Sam is out and the team is taking her to the hospital. She is in rough shape but will make a full recovery, physically at least anyway. I smile, it's comforting to know I have someone like Deano in my corner, no matter what.

'Thank you for this. Make sure you do the same, I'm always here for you and your team.'

A few more seconds go past. 'Tell her how you feel. Don't keep it hidden. 'Till our next adventure together, my friend.'

I go to respond but he is already gone.

CHAPTER 29

REVENGE

It's been a big 48 hours since the rescue. I reached out to Sam's boss at the ASD and have been feeding them intel on everything the cartel has: People, houses, cars, drugs and money. All of it. They thought they were in pain before because of the attack Foresight conducted on them, but they had no idea how bad it could get. They are certainly starting to find out now. I'm leaving nothing unturned. They need to all pay, every one of them, for what they did.

I'm watching surveillance of the latest bust. More than thirty people arrested and millions of drugs confiscated. It is a bad week for these low-lifes. I'm only just getting started though, all of these thugs are just that; thugs. None of them are the bosses. I want them, not their goons. They would have ordered the attack on Sam, so they need to suffer for it. Money is what they value most, so I'm taking it all, every cent. I won't keep any of it, I'll donate it all to charities and let the blood money do something good.

Once I take all the money, I'll take their freedom with the General's help. It's a good deal for him. I'm doing what red tape and bureaucracy prevent him from doing, but he gets all the evidence and credit in the end. I get revenge; he gets very happy bosses. Win-win, if you ask me.

Sam is still in the hospital being guarded by the General's team. I have been keeping an eye on the place through the surveillance systems just to make sure the cartel doesn't try to attack her again. I don't think they have the resources left to attempt such an attack, but I'm not leaving it to chance. She is looking like she will have at least a few more days in the hospital. I want to see her but it's not safe for me or her so it's off the cards.

I'll just have to keep her safe from a distance and enact revenge on her attackers. I know we are essentially still enemies, but I think we are slowly moving past that. I also don't know if she would still arrest me if she had the opportunity. She might give me a head start for saving her life, but she is very principled. She could arrest me just on that. I'm getting distracted again, seems to be happening a lot these last few days. I find myself watching her or letting my mind wander to thoughts of her. I need to pull myself together. We will never happen. We are from different worlds.

I focus my attention back on the job at hand. I have been tracking the three figureheads of the cartel for the last few hours. It would seem they are trying to go to ground but it has worked out worse for them as before I didn't know where they were but now they have revealed themselves to me. I'm tracking them via borrowed satellite resources from a couple of foreign governments, but I'm sure they won't mind me taking them for a little spin.

The cartel's money is almost completely gone and their resources are getting smaller by the minute. Once I have the final locations of the leaders, I'll hand over everything to General James and let the ASD do their thing with these guys. It will be a good day when they are all behind bars but I don't think it will be long before new figureheads try to take over. It will be hard for them though, with most of the original members all sitting behind bars looking at very lengthy sentences.

As long as Sam is safe though, that's all that matters to me. I have a feeling whoever comes out on top of the cartel after all of this will think twice about messing with any of us. We are not alone, but an army that can strike them on all fronts. The cost of further conflict would not be in their best interests. Maybe in years to come, when the memory of this fades, they might get the courage to come at us again, but I think it is unlikely.

I just need to focus on cleaning out the old guard and allow the dust to settle on what was once a very powerful cartel. I can see on the satellites that my targets have all arrived at their separate hiding places. They probably thought if they split up it would ensure at least one of them would survive this, but they still have no idea who they are up against. They underestimated the cost of their revenge. It was probably just about saving face with other crime families—they didn't want to appear weak or unable to defend themselves after Foresight struck them such a savage blow. I bet they regret worrying about their ego now.

I do some reconnaissance on the sites, doing as I do best, breaking into anything that is connected to the outer world. Two of the sites are easy. They have connected surveillance systems that basically allow me to just walk on in. The third site is a bit trickier, they seem to have been smart enough to keep it offline, but I can see several people at the location have mobile phones, which could be my in. I look for something in the area I could use to break the mobile phones or get some eyes on the property. Then, online, I see it, a drone flight school no more than a mile away. Oh, this could be fun.

I redirect the satellite to the area and can see on the imagery there are more than one hundred drones at the event.

'Sarina, I need to get control of the mobile tower network in that area. I need to remote hack and commandeer all of those drones. I think it's time we have some fun and send a swarm to meet the boss.'

It only takes Sarina and me a few minutes to secure the access I need. I execute a remote control override hack on all the drones at once. It only takes minutes; they aren't protected from this type of hack. Honestly, there wouldn't be too many situations where you would have this type of thing happen. It's pretty simple, I use the drones' systems update function to push my new variant of the software. I had to put together a version that would work with a few different brands but generally they have a similar base code, so it wasn't too difficult.

I can see the confusion for the crowd. They have all lost control of the drones and I have launched them all into the sky at once. Sarina, take control of the drones and make them a cohesive swarm. It looks impressive from the satellite view, hundreds of drones all in sync now heading towards the target.

I reach out to the General, inform him of the two locations ready for attack and read him in on the third site about to be attacked by a drone swarm. I had to tell him twice. He was a little surprised at my plan. He has teams ready to go and is mobilising them. They will all strike in one sweep. This is it, time to cut off the heads. I hand over access to the surveillance systems so they have eyes inside on the two locations. It will make it safer for them to sweep if they know who is where.

The third site strike team will converge on the target once the swarm attack is complete. The drones arrive over the site and I initiate a swarm brute force attack on all electronic devices. It's only seconds before I can gain access to mobile phones, TVs, solar systems, everything. It's surprising how much power this number of drones combined has. I initiate remote video and audio on all mobiles so I can hear everything as well as see the targets in a few instances. They can hear the swarm overhead. I can see them trying to figure out what the hell it is.

The strike team is now in place. It's time to create a real-life nightmare for my friends.

'Sarina, let's send in the drones. I want to break every window. Once they are broken, send the drones inside. See if we can take down some of these goons with the drones before the team moves in.'

Windows smash and I hear screaming and yelling. I guess this is probably very nightmarish. More than one hundred drones smashing through every possible entry point, blades spinning and all converging on your location. Yeah, that would scare the hell out of almost anyone. I wonder what is going through their minds.

A few seconds go by and I see most of the drones exit the building. 'Sir, all targets are down and the strike team is moving in. What do you want to do with the drones?'

I think about it for a few seconds. 'Sarina, return them to the owners. Once they are on the ground, initiate factory resets on all of them.'

The remaining swarm redirects and heads back to the field.

It's done. I took down the cartel. They are all behind bars. Sam is safe, at least from these thugs. Who knows who else she has pissed off though. Maybe I should do some digging and get ahead of the next revenge attack.

CHAPTER 30

FLOWERS

It's been almost a week now since Sam's rescue, she is getting out of the hospital today and her father is going to be taking her home. I think he is very worried about her. I see him hovering around the hospital, fussing over her, making sure she is comfortable and safe. He barely left the hospital the whole time she was in there. I think the only reason he did was to shower and have a bit of sleep. He didn't go to work or do anything other than be with her. He is a good dad.

I want to get her something, some sort of get well soon gift. Maybe a delivery or something to her house after she gets home this morning. I think she could do with some cheering up after everything that has happened. Maybe I could just send some flowers. She seemed to like that last time. I jump on a florist site near her home. Roses, nothing but the best. I click on the roses link and there are more than ten choices of colours.

I realise I don't know her favourite colour. I will need to do some digging and find out what she likes if I am going to keep sending her flowers. I don't know what is right and wrong here. I'll just get assorted ones. That should be easy, but how many should I get? I don't want to look cheap but I don't want to overdo it either. Oh hell, who cares, she was tortured just under a week ago. I think she has earnt a bit over the top. One thousand roses, that ought to cheer her up. Maybe a bit over the top, even in this circumstance, but what the hell. Big gestures and all that.

I enter the number and add a message for her. Nothing too sappy, can't have her thinking I have gone too soft on her. '*I hope you have a quick recovery. I'm looking forward to continuing our game.*' Although, what do I think 1k roses is saying? Mixed messages, Shadow. Mixed messages. I pay for the order with a secure payment method she can't track back to me. I am almost certain she will check if she can use it to track me. I wonder what she will think when she gets them.

I have been monitoring the house since she got home, just to make sure she is safe and I see the flowers getting delivered. Wow, okay, it turns out a thousand roses is a *lot* of flowers. Is she going to be a little weirded out by all of this? What will she tell her dad? Probably as little as possible. I don't think she will know what is going on. *I* don't know what is going on between us.

It takes them about fifteen minutes to carry all the bouquets into the house. The house is going to be full of flowers and toilet paper. I certainly like to deliver things in bulk. It's the thought that counts and as long as the flowers put a small smile on her face, that's all I want.

CHAPTER 31

BREAKING THE RULES

With most of the cartel now behind bars and the last few stragglers picked up this morning, the General has taken off the security detail from Sam's house. She is safe and I can move on, disappear into the shadows like I was never here. I think it's time I do. It's the best thing for Sam.

I just keep thinking about her though. I can't get her out of my head. Maybe I could drop by and say goodbye in person, now the security detail on her house has been removed. It would be safe enough for me to do it and Sarina could keep watch for anything suspicious while I'm inside. I know I really shouldn't, that it's a risk I shouldn't take, but I have to see her again in person, just this once. Then I'll walk away, disappear forever.

'Sarina, it's time to take a drive. Prepare the fleet. I want to ensure I'm not walking into a trap. I need your eyes, metaphorically speaking anyway, watching my back.' I check my outfit in the mirror and decide I should probably change my shirt. It looks a bit dishevelled. Maybe I'll fix my hair while I'm at it. After a few minutes of prepping, I head out to the car.

'Is everything ready?' I climb into the driver's seat and put my seatbelt on.

'Yes, everything is ready. The other vehicles are already enroute and will be able to give us the all clear before we arrive.' I chuckle to myself. Sarina already knows where we are going without me even telling her. Maybe I'm more predictable than I thought.

The drive is quick. It seems like no time at all and we are turning into Sam's street.

'How are we looking Sarina, are we clear to continue?'

A few moments go by as the car pulls up in front of Sam's house.

'Everything looks clear. No government vehicles or police in the area. I'll continue to monitor while you are inside and communicate through your earpiece if we need to make a quick exit.'

I open the car door and make my way up the path to the door. I reach out and knock. I wait, keeping an eye on my surroundings but it all still looks good. Suddenly the door opens and John, Sam's dad, is in front of me.

'Can I help you?'

I feel a bit nervous all of a sudden.

'Yes, I'm Jacob. I was wondering if I could talk to Sam for a few minutes?'

He raises a bushy eyebrow and looks at me with a judging glance. I don't blame him for being hesitant after what has happened.

'Sorry, I don't think that will be possible. She's still resting. You might need…' He trails off, looking behind him towards the stairs. It sounds like she is coming down herself. 'It looks like you are in luck; she's coming down. How about you wait in the lounge room and I'll tell her you're waiting.'

He gestures for me to go into the lounge and I do as he asks. I take a seat on the couch off to one side and wait for Sam. I need to pull myself together. I can take down a criminal syndicate without any concern at all, but meeting with Sam makes me a nervous wreck. A few minutes go by and I can hear Sam and John talking just outside the lounge room. Here she comes. She enters the room and I stand to greet her.

'Good morning, Sam. You look like you're improving.' It looks like she is a bit surprised to see me standing in her lounge room. 'I wanted to check on you before I move on, make sure you were recovering well. It looks like you are.' She is wearing baggy tracksuit pants and a t-shirt. Very casual and maybe a little daggy, but I still think she looks amazing. I see her check her outfit and almost try to straighten up a little. 'I was very sorry all that happened to you, that is not something I would like you to have experienced. I didn't see them coming. I'm sorry for that.'

I think she is a little confused, trying to figure out, like me, what this is between us, what is happening here. She steps forward, closing the gap slightly. I am not sure if it's to be closer to me, or so she can talk to me without her dad overhearing our conversation.

'Why are you here? Why did you save me?'

That's good, at least she isn't thinking about arresting me. Well, not right now anyway.

'I'm here to see you, silly.' I smile slightly and take a step closer towards her. 'You already know why I saved you. I like you Sam and I think you like me too?'

Her expression changes, she looks almost angered by my words. Is it because it is true, does she like me and is trying to deny it to herself?

She seems to shake it off. 'Don't be ridiculous. I don't like you like that. You are my target. I'm going to arrest you. Not today—I owe you that at least, but I'll find you and I'll arrest you.'

I take another step towards her. I want to kiss her. Those lips, that smile, those eyes. I take another step forward so I'm right in front of her.

'What are you doing?'

Our proximity seems to be making her a little nervous, if the blush creeping up her neck is anything to go by. I smile at her for a second, holding her gaze.

'I wanted to make sure you were safe. Your team is busy with the last of the intel I sent through to them. They will have the remaining members of the cartel in minutes if they don't mess it up. I can't stay long, I just wanted to say goodbye. I am truly looking forward to our next game of skill.' I look into her eyes and continue to hold her gaze. She is beautiful. I have never met anyone like her. She doesn't look away. If I'm going to kiss her, now is my chance. I lean forward slowly, giving her plenty of time to back away if she's not interested.

Soft, gentle lips meet mine. She responds, not resisting my kiss. I slide my hand around her waist, pulling her closer. I'm mindful of her injuries, careful not to hurt her. I lose myself in the kiss. I'm completely consumed by the moment. Every cell in my body feels like it is charged and my every sense is heightened. I want more. I don't want this to end, but it must, I know it must.

I pull back slowly and her eyes are closed. She is as lost in the moment as I was. Her eyes open slowly. I just look at her for a few more moments. Neither of us say anything; there's not enough words for what I'm feeling.

I clear my throat and take a step back. 'Goodbye Sam.'

I walk out of the house. That will be the last time I see her. My heart sinks in my chest at the thought. I walk down the path and get into the waiting car. As soon as the door closes it accelerates quickly down the street. I can still taste her on my lips.

Leaving is going to be harder than I thought.

CHAPTER 32

MOVING ON

I'm struggling with leaving Sam behind. I know I needed to do it. It's the best thing for her and me, but I hate it. Work, that's what I need. I need to distract myself with something big, something that will take up all my effort. It needs to be epic, otherwise I'll just get bored and start to mope around again thinking about Sam, Foresight, all of the above. They are separate but the same, beautiful, powerful and a little terrifying, if I'm honest, but in all the right ways.

Yes, she is beautiful but it is so much more than that. She has this aura around her, a sense of power and strength that draws me in. Her skills as a hacker are undeniably impressive. I don't believe I have met anyone that could hold a candle to her. She is almost perfect, if there is such a thing.

Wow, I'm doing it again, letting my mind wander to her.

Distraction, I need to find one fast. Who is the biggest, baddest, baddie other than the cartel? There has to be someone. A whisper, something, *anything* to occupy my thoughts.

'Sarina, start a search on the dark web forums and marketplaces. Find me the devil, someone or something whispered about in the cesspit of the internet. Find me someone evil to take down, one worthy of my skills.' I see the servers all come to life in the bunker rack. Sarina is kicking into high gear. I hope it doesn't take her too long to find me a target.

It takes a few hours before Sarina has a list for me of potential targets, many would-be hackers or criminals. Even a few plain old con artists. As I look through the list, I'm a little disappointed. I get it, these people are scum and the world would be better off without them. My time would be worthwhile eradicating them, but none of them would be of great challenge. I need a challenge. Then, towards the end of the list, I see it.

Arachnid.

A hacking group that looks to be made up of 15-twenty members, if they are all still active.

They steal money from everyone, charities, governments, anyone they can, it doesn't matter. They just take it all, ruining lives in their wake. They even help terrorists if the money is right. They are good too, not individually like Sam or myself but as a group, they truly have some skills. Enough to certainly keep me on my toes. Hopefully this will help me forget about Sam.

I get to work, digging into the group. I need to find everything I can. I do it gently though, I don't want to tip them off. That would ruin my surprise and certainly make it harder to inflict real pain. I start by putting together the pieces, the individual members. I want to know who I'm up against.

I dredge through everything I can find on them. I have confirmed at least ten members with a potential eight more who I can't specifically pin anything on. They really are black hats. Nothing they do is for anyone but themselves; they just care about money and power. They sound just like any other low life criminal, except these thugs hide behind the keyboard and help fund terrorist groups if the money trail is accurate.

It looks like it's just when it's of benefit to them, or they need influence somewhere, but helping terrorists is still helping terrorists. I need to go after the money and do it quietly. That's what will hurt them the most but they will strike back, of that I'm certain.

I found the usual accounts in the Caymans, a few million, but the real money is sitting in two crypto accounts. I need to find a way to get the keys for these wallets. Both accounts appear to be controlled by one member of the group. He must be like the financial controller of the group, in charge of funnelling the cash when it is needed by the members. It is all about lavish lifestyles: cars, boats, houses. They cause so much pain to their victims just so they can drive nice cars and eat caviar.

I could have been like these people. I really could have, not caring about who was in my way just doing what I wanted. I was heading down that path, caring less about who and what my targets were. My revenge for my parents has long been my fuel but I seem to be shifting my focus. Sam seems to be my new compass. She has helped me refocus and makes me want to try to do better, *be* better.

Every time I close my eyes I see her, remember our kiss. The softness of her lips, the gentle aroma of her hair. It's vivid, like we are still there, connecting, gently, passionately. I want to be deserving of her.

Focus, Shadow. Focus.

So much for a distraction.

Bank accounts, let's get the crypto accounts. To gain access to his accounts I'll need to get the password somehow. I can see he frequents a café in Rome. At the same time, once a week, he takes a laptop and orders something to eat. He does something on the laptop after he eats, but nothing connected to him personally. He wouldn't be much of a hacker if he wasn't anonymising his activities, so it doesn't surprise me I can't find any activity. The footage from the café security I access shows he does something on a mobile phone.

Maybe it is an encrypted device. Maybe it houses the keys I need.

How can I get access to that phone though? I can't just stroll up to him in Rome and say, 'Hey, can I borrow your phone for a minute?'

Maybe I could crack the phone using a drone. I could launch it from nearby and crack the phone from above his location. The drone would be easy to organise. I could just purchase a specially modified one on the dark web. They would even deliver and retrieve it at my desired location. I have time. If the routine stays as it is, he will be at the café tomorrow, midday. That should be plenty of time to prepare.

I have my plan. Time to get organised.

I go to one of the main dark web marketplaces and reach out to a seller with my requirements, one which I have used before. It only takes a few minutes to get a response and I pay the stipulated fee. There isn't much point in arguing about the price, it's reasonable and the timeframe is tight. I need the workmanship to be spot on, so it's worth the cost. It will be on location tomorrow, about thirty minutes before the café opens. It will be activated and sitting on an easy release charger, allowing it to stay online and be ready to launch when it is needed. It will be encrypted with a private key sent to me beforehand, allowing secure uninterrupted communications via a private 5G internet service connected to the customised Raspberry Pi mounted on the top of the drone in a specialised case. A booster aerial will ensure maximum range on the device.

I have gained access to the street camera systems and the café network. They have a poor quality camera setup, but it will help keep me in the loop of what is happening around the target. It's time to get some rest. I'll need to be on my game tomorrow to be able to get away with hacking a hacker's phone, stealing their crypto wallets, and actually getting away with it all undetected.

Wow, it sounds a lot harder when I put it that way. I can do it though, piece of cake. I hope…

CHAPTER 33

TROUBLE

It's almost 7:30 pm Brisbane time, which is almost 11:30 am in Rome. I need to get ready; my target is going to be arriving soon. I connect up to the drone and test spin all the blades. I don't lift it off the charging pad as I want it to have a full charge when we start. It's got a bit of an extra load with the Raspberry Pi on top. All systems are a go. I connect to the Pi and see what platform has been preconfigured for me. It's a version of Kali, which is good, it will make my job even easier.

I update all the packages on Kali to ensure I have the latest versions of the tools. I pull down some custom exploit packages, including the cyberpunk777 package, which will allow me to exploit the android phone on my target. Well, that's the plan anyway. I'm going to use meterpreter to push the package and initiate the command and control of the phone. I generate a custom version of the WiFi pineapple, I think it would have to be one of my favourite WiFi hacking platforms. It's simple and reliable, which is perfect for this type of scenario. I really don't want to be half way through and have the platform jam up on me. It will let me connect and intercept the café WiFi. Hopefully, I'll get access to the laptop, but that's a bit of a long shot. It is worth a try though to see what else

I can get from our unsuspecting hacker.

I'm ready. It's almost noon now and I see the target approaching as predicted. I launch the drone high above the café, high enough so it can't be easily seen or heard. I test video systems' capability: no problems found. Everything is functioning as desired and I have a clear line of sight to the target from above. I have to be careful to have enough height and distance so no one will hear the drone, but close enough to be able to use the tools effectively.

I initiate the scan for the mobile devices. I can see three mobile devices, one android and two iPhones. That makes narrowing them down easy. From his social media I can see he's a committed android user. I fire up meterpreter and engage the device. It takes only a few moments to initiate the exploit package and gain an SSH connection. I'm in. I initiate a full data transfer to the Pi. As soon as it completes, I'll export it back to my systems.

A few moments pass and it completes.

'Sarina, transfer the data from the target's phone into a containerised secure storage, just in case it's a trap. Once it is secure, I need you to find me the crypto wallet keys.' I turn my attention to the WiFi network. I initiate the pineapple instance I created and force a reconnection of all devices on the WiFi network, setting up my instance as the new primary base station. I capture all of the authentication handshakes and use one of them to authenticate on the network. I do a light scan on the network, nice and gentle, not to give myself away. I find the target's machine.

I initiate a meterpreter exploit on the laptop, surprisingly, it is not patched and I just walk through the door. It is like he held the door open for me. A hacker should know better. Is this a honeypot, to lure me into a trap? This is way too easy. No, I don't think it is. I'm pretty certain they don't even know I'm here. I think hackers are probably a little like mechanics. Mechanics don't always look after their cars like they recommend for customers. The last thing they want to do most times when they knock off is work on another car, so it gets ignored. Same for a hacker. They break or protect systems all day depending on what side of the fight they are on and they don't look after their systems like they probably should. Funny how that works. You could probably say the same for chefs, accountants, tailors, or any profession really.

'Sir, I have found the keys you are looking for. The two wallets combined have a total of around 890k in bitcoin. Do you want to initiate a transfer and wash the funds?'

Wow, they are not going to be happy when they discover I took all of that.

'Yes, initiate a clean of the funds.' I watch the funds drain from the wallets and start to transfer in pieces across thousands of other wallets. Even I can't tell where it is all going and I'm watching it in real-time. Thousands of small transfers to thousands of different wallets. It then gets transferred out into an unidentifiable bank account in US dollars.

$890k in bitcoin doesn't sound like much, but when you transfer it out into USD it is over $35 billion and that's after the washing losses. That's the life savings of the group; the blood money they have hurt so many people to get.

Sarina is fast. The wash only takes a few minutes. I have never seen that much money. Have I gone too far? These thugs are not going to let that kind of money go. Even the cartel only had hundreds of millions, not billions like this. I'll have to ensure I can't be found, make sure I have no trace.

The exploit on the laptop was a success. Should I back away, quit while I'm ahead? I have already taken everything from them. They will have to start again if they can't find me and get the money back. They have no money and no power left. Yes, they are all still hackers and I'm sure they could easily rustle up a few more million pretty easily between them in a few days so it is unlikely they will lose any of their fancy homes or cars, but this kind of hit will be very ego bruising.

I have a strong feeling our poor financial controller will end up somewhere in a ditch. It wasn't my intention but a cold reality in the world he runs in. They will be looking to save face and punish someone for this.

No, I won't walk away. I'll finish what I started. I connect to the machine and initiate a remote data transfer as I did with the phone. The data is flowing across to the drone quickly and I'm almost finished when the connection is severed. He has detected my activity. The game is up. I really should have just walked away with the money and disappeared. Instead, I was reckless, and now it could cost me. I need to clean and cover my tracks.

'Sarina, pull any data we just received over into another secure storage area. I'll review the data later. Infect the device and encrypt the laptop. Go loud with the attack. He already knows we're here, so it won't matter.' I give Sarina a few minutes before I send the drone off onto a random roof and initiate a remote wipe. I start to wash my tracks when I see something on my network.

He has followed the file transfer.

How? I was clean. This is not the time for mistakes, not the time at all.

It's only a few more minutes and I can see a huge influx of activity hitting the outside of my network. They are trying to push their way in.

'Sarina, push them back and make it so they fear us. Hit them all hard. Let's see what they're made of.'

Sarina hits them with almost everything we have, the full power of the bunker's resources. It's powerful but I'm not sure it will be enough. The attack stops and everything goes quiet.

A few minutes go by before a message pops up on one of the underground chat boards directed at me. I guess they know who I am.

You stole from the wrong people, Shadow. You might be good but we will make you pay. We will hunt you and everyone you love. You will all suffer. Enjoy the money why you can still breathe.

Wow, that's a little dramatic. I drum my fingers on my keyboard. They don't seem to be messing around. I think I made a big mistake and I'm going to need some help…

CHAPTER 34

ASKING FOR HELP

I'm a little nervous about how today is going to go. Will she be willing to help me? Or will she A: arrest me or B: flat out refuse to help. It could easily be either, most likely B, as I could still carry some favour with her over the rescue, but that will wear out eventually, unless she does like me. She didn't stop me when I kissed her, after all, she even seemed to reciprocate.

I have had Sarina search Sam out. She and her team are about to conduct a surveillance op in Brisbane city. Someone selling stolen data or something, that doesn't matter to me though, I just care about the fact she is going to be out in the open. I need to figure out how I can arrange a conversation with her. I make my way into the city with the fleet, just in case I need to switch rides a few times on my exit. I will send in one of the other cars initially to scoop up Sam and lose any tails if needed before I join her in the car. I can easily watch from one of the other cars and keep at a safe distance.

I watch the exchange take place and then the teams break off. The main group follows the foreign agent and Sam wanders off slowly down the street, casually keeping an eye on the way over to their head seller, who is going to have a really bad day. I don't think it will be long before they drag him in for interrogation. This is my chance to get her alone.

'Sarina, take the Tesla and stop her midway across the pedestrian crossing. Once she is stopped, wait for her to get in.'

I watch Sarina come to an aggressive stop right in front of Sam. It would appear she is startled by the sudden appearance of the car and takes a few steps back. I can see her looking at the car, confused. I get out my phone and type a message to Sam: *Get in.* Simple, straight to the point.

Sam takes her phone out of her pocket while others walk around the car blocking the crossing. She just keeps looking at the message, I guess deciding if she wants to go down this path. I don't have time for this. I repeat my message: *Get in, Sam.*

She steps forward after a few seconds, deciding to go with it. She grabs the handle and slides into the back seat.

'Sarina, take her a few suburbs away and set up a rendezvous point so I can get in the car with her.' As soon as her door closes, the car surges to life. I wonder what Sam thinks of the no driver, it can be quite terrifying the first time. I still sometimes have the urge to take over, but honestly, Sarina is probably a better driver than I am.

Almost twenty minutes go by and I get out of my car just before an intersection. I'll get in the car at the traffic lights. Sarina will make sure the lights are red long enough to allow me to enter the car. I make my way over to the lights and I can see several cars approaching the intersection, including Sam in the Tesla. The lights turn red and the cars come to a stop, my turn to make my entrance. I step out onto the street, walking directly towards the car. I take a deep breath. Here we go. I grab the handle and slide in the car next to Sam.

As I enter the car and close the door, I can see Sam watching me. She looks unsure about the situation, looking at the door, almost reaching for the door handle. She is furrowing her eyebrows a little. I know this kind of situation is probably not one she would feel very comfortable in after what she has gone through. Random people just jumping into the car at an intersection would not make her feel very safe at all. I'm impressed though, as she looks like she is handling this very well. As soon as the door closes, the car surges forward at a sudden speed. Sarina is getting some distance from anyone who could be trying to follow us.

'Sarina, change Tesla one's colour to grey, avoid surveillance zones.' I see Sam look at me with a very confused look, a judgemental furrow of sorts, like what drugs is this guy on, a car can't just change colour or drive by itself. I watch her closely as Sarina initiates the change on the cars nanoshell. Sam looks in awe of what is happening, her eyes are wide with fascination and wonder. If she doesn't arrest me, I'm certain I'll be spending some time explaining about the car and Sarina, but for now, I have pressing matters we need to discuss.

'I missed you Sam. You look good.' She holds my gaze. I know, I know, pressing matters and all I want to do is say I missed her? Get a hold of yourself, Shadow.

A few more moments go by and she folds her arms over her chest. 'So, what is this all about? What do you want?'

I'm a little thrown by her directness and my stomach twists into knots. I take a deep breath. 'I need your help...' I take another breath. 'I've gotten myself into a bit of a situation. I was trying to distract myself and went after a criminal hacking group called Arachnid. I think I may have bitten off more than I can chew.'

Her eyebrow quirks, 'What did you do? What sort of trouble are you in?'

I look her in the eyes and get lost in them for a moment. She looks away. Oh no. I'm starting to make this a little awkward.

'Sorry. I went after the group's money, the thing they value most. I have taken it all. A total of around 35 billion, which is ridiculous on its own, but these people are the worst of our world. They work with terrorists and steal from everyone. They honestly don't care who they hurt in the process. It is just about power and money.' I stop and look out the window for a moment before looking back at her. She seems to have softened a little and relaxed.

'So basically, you set fire to a wolf pack's cave and are now being hunted by them? Is that about right?'

Her smile takes me by surprise. She is having a dig at me. 'Yes, I guess that's what I did. I know, probably not the smartest move I have ever made.'

She shakes her head. 'No, probably not.' She pauses, 'Look, I know I owe you for saving me from the cartel. What do you want me to do?'

I need to explain that even if she doesn't help me, she could still be in danger. I don't want that to influence her choice but she needs to know.

'I want you to team up with me, to help me defeat them. Bring the criminals to justice and hopefully save my bacon at the same time.'

She turns and looks out the window, I assume considering her options.

'There is more, Sam. They threatened to come after everyone I love: my friends, my family, everyone. Apart from Sarina, you are the only person I communicate with regularly. If they find any trace of our hacker's duel, you will become a target. Whether you decide to help me or not, you will need to watch on your six.'

She continues to look out the window for what seems like minutes when in reality it may have just been seconds. She finally turns to look me in the eyes.

'If I help you, the money will need to become the property of ASD. You can't keep any of it.' I nod, I'd expected that. 'I'll also need to do this with ASD's support. I won't go rogue to help you. That could mean you may be arrested and although I owe you, I may not be able to prevent that.'

'I can live with that. Preferably not the jail part, but if that is how it plays out, then so be it.' I hold her gaze. 'If we're going to work together, there's something else I think we should discuss… The kiss.' Sam gets a little colour to her cheeks and shifts uncomfortably in her seat.

'How about we focus on the current problem before we make this more complicated.' I nod, willing to let the subject drop, for now. 'I'll need to go back to the General to get permission to move forward. Can you get this car of yours to take me back to where you picked me up?'

'Sarina, return Sam to the location you picked her up.' The car pulls over and does a U-turn. We are making our way back. We don't say anything further on the ride back but we both continue to steal looks at each other. I want to say something more to her, tell her how I feel, but she's right, we need to focus on the problem first. I could be going to jail after all of this plays out, so one step at a time.

The car arrives and she turns to look at me. 'I'll come back to you with ASD's answer. Don't do anything stupid in the meantime.'

CHAPTER 35

WAITING FOR MY ANSWER

It has been more than 24 hours since I met with Sam. If I close my eyes, I can almost smell the fruity scent of her hair products. The sweet hint floating in the air, just enough to fill my senses sitting next to her in the back seat of the car. The memory constantly drifts into my mind. I don't care. There is no keeping her out anymore, she is a constant. Everything is quiet on both fronts, with no further action from Arachnid or any communication from Sam. I'll assume Sam is trying to convince the General that it is in ASD's interest to work with me to bring down this group.

Arachnid, I'm certain, will be hunting me. Trying to dig into who I am, what I have done and ultimately find where I'm hiding. It won't be an easy job though, not many people in this world have the skills to find me, to find the mistakes I have made. Sam for sure, but I'm hoping she is on my side. I guess I just need to wait and see how this all plays out.

I need to be prepared either way. If Sam can't or won't help, I'll need to figure out how to defeat Arachnid. It won't be easy, especially alone, but I have to come up with something.

'Sarina, we need to find every asset connected to the members of Arachnid. We also need to find enemies of theirs, potentially other hackers who do not show them favour, any that may help my cause.' If Sam doesn't get involved, I'll certainly have enough money to pay them for their assistance, but I would prefer to work with Foresight, not random hackers I don't trust.

I should consider reaching out to Deano. I might need his help if things go south. I pick up my phone and send a quick text to Deano: *Are you still in the area? I have got myself in a bit of a situation and may need your help.* I go to put the phone back in my pocket when I feel the vibration of a new message. That was fast.

For you my friend—we are at the ready.

Well, that is something. I have protection if I need it. I need to remember I'm working against a group that works with terrorists, so you never know what might happen.

I get to work creating some new custom attack tools, updating some of my custom malware. I have to be on my game or they will wipe the floor with me. I also need to be able to hold my own with Sam. I have no doubt she is the better of us, but I don't want to look useless. I already feel like a nervous schoolboy around a pretty girl, so I don't want to lose the one part of me I know can offer her some strength, some skill.

I start to see a list of properties connected with Arachnid. There is property all over the world. They certainly had a great lifestyle, jetsetting around, flaunting their money to the world as though they are rich, bratty socialites. You know the type, they inherit all their family's wealth and burn through their trust funds like it means absolutely nothing. It suits them, if you ask me.

The ASD will love this list if they come on board, it will provide an impressive proceeds of crime seizure list. It will net some great profit when they auction it all off, which is allowed as a fundraising exercise. Although I don't think they will have any budget or cash flow issues with the $35 billion injection of funds I liberated from

Arachnid. It's a pretty sweet power they have, that allows them to transfer ownership of all seized assets. Bad news for criminals, but great for agencies like ASD. Having a few budget constraints? Go seize some drug lord's assets. Budget issues solved.

I start to pace, back and forth, back and forth. It is starting to drive me crazy not knowing what is going to happen. Will I get to work with her? I hope I do. I'm both excited and terrified about the idea. She makes me so nervous, I'm a complete mess around her. I fumble through each conversation and make things a awkward on occasion by holding her gaze a little too long.

I really need to get that under control. I am supposed to be this scary, shadowy hacker that scares would-be-hackers in the dark recesses of the internet. Why can I not keep it together with Foresight?

'Sir, the list is complete. I included all motor vehicle and marine assets to ensure you have an accurate list.' I glance over the completed list. They have yachts, sports cars, mansions and even an island, by the looks of it. What a way to live. I guess it was good for them while it lasted. I'll make sure they are all finished, all behind bars in some dingy cell. That's what they deserve. The first thing though is survival and then I'll go on the offensive to finish what I started.

My phone starts to vibrate in my pocket. It's a message from Sam. *Meet me in 1 hour, the same place you picked me up yesterday. Don't be late.* I guess it is time to find out my fate.

'Sarina, get the car ready. We have a date with Sam in an hour.'

CHAPTER 36

THE ARRANGEMENT

We are nearly at the rendezvous spot, the crossing in the city. The sweet smell of Sam's hair flows into my mind, almost like a craving. My mind and body long for her to be close. Wow, okay I need to reel that back in, I need to focus on the mission. This is going to be dangerous. Someone will get hurt if I can't bring everything I have to the table. I need to be present and on mission. Our lives could depend on it.

The car comes around the corner and I see her standing by the side of the intersection. I lose my breath at the sight of her for a moment. Get it together. Get your mind on the mission. I'm starting to feel like a caveman who would club his potential mate over the head and drag them back to his dingy cave to enjoy a fire-roasted dinosaur leg. That is a far stretch from a super-elite, feared, underground hacker type. A super intelligent and supposedly modern man who should be able to get a grip of his thoughts and emotions long enough to have an intelligent conversation. Seriously, get a grip, she's just a girl.

Sarina brings the car to a steady stop next to Sam and she climbs in next to me. As soon as the door closes, the car starts to drive at a relaxed pace.

'Good morning,' she says. She watches me for a few moments

before looking in the front of the car. 'You are going to have to explain all of this to me. Maybe introduce me to your car?' I smile. She has no idea about Sarina, how powerful she is and real she is. I wonder if they will get along.

Weirdly, I have concerns if my artificial intelligence girl, Sarina, is going to get along with Sam, the ASD agent hacker who is hunting me and will likely arrest me when all this is over. Who knew that could ever be a thing, a reality, not just a figment of my imagination? What a strange situation I have gotten myself into.

I have never shown Sarina to anyone before, but for the first time, I feel like I want to show Sam what I'm capable of, what wonders we could create together. I've barely brushed the surface with Sarina's capability, she could be truly amazing. The only limitation is the hardware she runs on but I have noticed that the more I allow her to do her own thing the more she seems to flourish. She utilises power from anywhere she interacts and is not limited to the original servers I have given her. She is evolving and developing, almost like a child. I'm watching her grow in front of me, developing her potential.

I'll need to be careful though, I don't want Sarina to be taken by the ASD. They would abuse her abilities, corrupting her true purpose. That is not a now problem to solve though, I need to focus on Sam. I look over and she is watching me. She doesn't look at me like I'm the enemy anymore, she is just trying to figure me out.

'I think I could share some secrets with you. Once our current business is concluded.' She nods and I continue, 'You look nice today.' She blushes but recovers quickly.

'Let's not get distracted. We have important things to discuss.' I nod and she continues, 'I have discussed your situation with the General at great length and he is willing to call, let's say, a temporary truce. He feels it is in all of our interests to eradicate this group and he was impressed at how helpful you were at bringing down the cartel. There are some rules and stipulations on his agreement though.' She watches for my reaction.

'I thought there might be at least a few rules or requirements. One of them is the funds, I'm guessing?'

She nods. 'Yes, that is correct. All funds will need to become the property of ASD, but he indicated we have authority to use it during this mission to obtain anything we need. This will help ASD keep a 'no knowledge' of the operation stance. That is the second stipulation: this will be a black op, no official connection to ASD and if we get caught, they will deny all knowledge of the operation. Are you okay with that?'

I nod. That's what I was already expecting. 'So, what happens to me if we make it through this mess?'

She looks away, I don't think this is going to be an answer I want to hear. 'The General indicated he would consider what you have done and what this operation will do, when deciding your fate, but he wouldn't give an answer for if you would be arrested or not. You may get a reduced sentence but I don't think you will avoid jail time completely. That's the risk you will need to bear if you accept my help, ASD's help.' She looks out the window and her voice is softer. 'I tried to barter for you. I owed you that much, but I wasn't able to get a definitive answer. I'm sorry.' I can tell it pains her she couldn't get me immunity, but she did her best. That's all I could ask of her.

'Thank you. I appreciate what you have done for me. I accept the terms of the agreement.' She smiles. I think she was hoping we would get to work together. I think that is one of the main reasons I'm not getting the hell out of here and finding an alternative way to solve this mess.

'So, what now?'

'I'll arrange a site to work from, a black site. We will need to access those funds to get the gear we will need to wage this war. Do you want to bring in my team to help, or do you want this to be just us?'

I think about it for a few moments. 'I think the three of us can handle it.'

She looks a little confused at the statement. 'Three of us? What do you mean *three* of us?'

I smile, she is going to get a kick out of this.

'Sarina, say hello to our new friend Sam, or Foresight, if you will.'

Sam looks at me like I'm losing my mind. If I was in her shoes, I would probably think that too.

'Hello, Foresight. I have seen a lot of your work. You are impressive. We are going to be good friends, I can feel it.'

CHAPTER 37

DOUBLE TEAM

It's been a few days since our arrangement was made and the girls met. Sarina was right, they are becoming good friends. Sam has even had some ideas on how to improve Sarina's hardware and ability to utilise outside resources while cloaking her from any external view. ASD has set up a black site just outside the city with a dual fibre backbone running into the site. We have acquired some very substantial servers and two desktops that would make any gamer weep with joy. The setup was expensive but, I have to say, very impressive.

Sarina is already integrated into the systems and has, in her own words, been tweaking them to gain full capability as well as allowing her full use as needed. I have to admit, I have enjoyed the last couple of days, building this all with Sam. She constantly surprises me by how capable and independent she is. Personal interests aside, she is a very impressive human, one I'm honoured to know and have this opportunity to work with. I'll have to make sure I tell her that before I get dragged away in cuffs.

'I think we are all set up. We are ready to get to work.'

Sam is under the desk, connecting everything together. She looks up at me. 'I think you are right. Sarina, can you please make sure all systems are up to date and do a full systems check?' She climbs out and looks at the screens in front of us.

A few seconds go by. 'Of course, Foresight, I'll start a full diagnostic immediately.'

Sam and Sarina seem to be working together really well. They seem to just click, like they know what each other is going to want next and just adapt as they interact.

'Let's get a bite to eat while we wait?'

I nod. We relax and eat a basic meal in the lounge area of the site. Sam puts on a movie, *Varsity Blues*, not a bad choice. We relax and enjoy each other's company. A bit of casual chat through the movie, one we have both seen quite a few times before. We are sitting close on the couch, sort of leaning towards each other, just mere centimetres away. I can almost feel the warmth from her skin on mine. Every nerve ending is firing, alert for any touch. It is electrifying, having her so close.

'Shadow, Foresight, the systems checks have all been completed. All custom tools and applications both of you utilise are loaded onto each of your systems and I have optimised myself for the upcoming activities. We are ready to work when you are.'

I jump at Sarina's voice, the intense moment with Sam interrupted. I glance at her and she looks excited to get to work, already starting to tidy the snacks away.

'Let's do it, Sam.'

We get up and put our dishes in the sink, grab some work supplies (energy drinks and potato chips for me and coke with snake lollies for Sam). We are ready to go now. We head back over to the desks and sit down. I look over at Sam and she is firing up her custom hunting tools she created to help find our targets. She must sense me watching her and looks over with a smile on her face.

'Shadow, you are getting distracted. Focus. I need you to focus.' I nod and she continues, 'You go after all of their remaining assets. We want to leave them with nothing, no money, no physical possessions, no friends to hide them. We want to make this uncomfortable for them. I'll hunt them down so we know where they all are. Once we have the information we need, we will double team them, one by one until we have eradicated their capability and sent in a strike team to arrest them.'

I get to work. I start with the money, any money I can find, anything they have hidden, I take it and add it to our collection. I repossess homes and cars; nothing is safe from us.

I'm nearing my goal when I hear Sam talking to Sarina, 'Sarina, please collate the list. Ensure you monitor the movements of all targets. We need to be ready for any sudden changes. It allows us to adapt or shift targets if needed.' She must be finished her tasks. She gets out of her chair and walks over to me, sits her arm on top of my chair and leans in to see where I'm up to. 'Do you need some help?' I suddenly get a whiff of the sweet perfume she is wearing, the almost fruity scent that's been haunting me these last few weeks. I breathe it in, letting it intoxicate my senses. I must have been absent for too long, enjoying my rush, because she digs an elbow into my ribs.

'Earth to Shadow, you still in there?'

I shake it off and hit enter on the last attack sequence.

'Done, all done. Within minutes the last of the assets will be repossessed and they will have nothing but what they can carry. They will bunker down. We need to prepare to strike the final blows.' She looks almost through me for a second, like she is completely lost in thought. After a few seconds, she refocuses.

'What's the rush? Let's take a break and let Sarina keep an eye on our new friends for a couple of hours. I'm going to take a shower and then it's your choice of movie.'

Sam and I have been staying at the ASD's black site since we started. Her dad thinks she is away on some training event. I really don't think he would approve if he knew what she was doing. The whole going after a dangerous cyber crime group and the sharing a place with me for a week, I hope he never finds out about either.

I don't argue with Sam. I don't think it would get me anywhere even if I did. She walks through to the other end of the site towards the bathroom, a few moments later, I hear the shower running. I try not to think about her in the shower and head over to get some snacks ready. Salted butter popcorn. I've learned Sam loves it and some large cups of coke zero. As I place the drinks down on the coffee table and reach for the remote to find us a movie, I see Sam come back into the room in the corner of my eye. She is dripping wet, with only a towel wrapped around her. I can't help but stare, completely enthralled by the vision before me.

She grins as she sees my expression. 'Sorry, I forgot my bag. What movie did you choose?'

I stumble with my thoughts. *Movie? What movie? Oh! I was supposed to choose a movie, wasn't I?*

'Umm I haven't found one yet. I just finished getting our snacks ready. Popcorn, just how you like it.'

She nods and grabs her bag from near the couch. 'Sounds great. I'll be out in a few minutes.' She turns and heads back out of sight at the other end of the house. I watch her as she leaves. *Wow, I need something a little stiffer to drink now.*

CHAPTER 38

FIRST ASSAULT

It is early in the morning. I can see the sunrise starting to come up over the horizon. Sam isn't up yet, I'm just sitting on the balcony drinking a cup of coffee thinking about last night. We finished getting ready for this morning's assault before sitting down and watching a movie together. By the end of the movie, Sam was leaning up against me. We were laughing and just enjoying ourselves. I don't even remember what movie I put on. We didn't really watch it, we talked and joked all the way through. It was just a backdrop to our conversation, filling in any blanks in the conversation, which were very few and far between. I want to remember last night if I do end up in custody after this, just enjoy the happiness I haven't felt since my parents died.

I hear Sam make a coffee and she makes her way out to me.

'Good morning, Sam. How did you sleep?'

She sips her coffee and smiles. 'Very well, thanks. I'm energised and excited to get to work. I think we are going to have some real fun today.'

I agree, it should be a good day. I have this strange feeling though, I can't put my finger on it but it's like we are missing something. We sit sipping our coffees watching the sunrise in front of us. It is a beautiful morning, a little chilly, but still beautiful.

We don't talk much, just sit and take it all in.

I'm startled back to focus by Sarina, 'Team, the main target is on the move. I have commandeered a spy drone from the ASD fleet and I'm tracking him on the move north from Perth. We should let the authorities pick him up and go after his second. They have been very active in the last 12 hours, drumming up support and securing new tools by the looks of things. We don't want them to build up too much support, so he is a good target.' We look over at each other, nod and get to our feet. It's time.

I review the reconnaissance Sam's completed on our target and what Sarina has added to the file. We have a few options here.

'Foresight, do you want to take the front door and smash down the building security systems, cut the external communications and water supplies? Or do you want to go after the target direct?'

She smiles at me, an almost mischievous look. 'I'll take the direct attack, thanks.'

With that said, I get to work. I start by looking at what I can see. Sarina has done a great job putting together all of the site details I need. I have IP addresses, domains, even how far away authorities are in case we need to hit abort and clear our tracks. They have the usual security cameras, open to the internet, not the smartest thing to do but everyone wants to be able to check from everywhere. Companies need to work on security by design, not a simple bolt-on later solution because customers are scared of getting hacked. It will help improve the horrible security they all have, except for the small few who care about security. At least they try. Even if it is not much better, they still tried. I disable the sensor alarms. I've exploited a few of the smart devices on the network, that should help us get some inside ears for the location.

I start to see a flood of activity hit the network. Foresight is in.

She is making a move, showing our target he should be scared. We are here to take him down. We will not show him any mercy. That usually makes people start to lose their cool. I see the defences start to come down. We are barely getting any resistance, it's a little strange. Pieces are falling to the wayside quickly. In a few minutes, they will be locked out of their systems and we can call the feds in. Then I see it, a slight spike in activity on our network. Maybe they are going to fight back a little, good, some fun at last.

The slight uptick turns to an avalanche. Multiple sources are targeting us. We look at each other, and I can see the horror in Sam's eyes.

We've made a mistake.

We thought we were in control of the situation and underestimated our opponent. They let us pick at them, inflict a little more pain. They wanted to track us, find out where we were and bring the assault to us. They are hunting us when we thought we were in pursuit of them. We have been played. It takes some serious strength and will to just sit, to let buzzards pick at your rotting flesh. I should have seen this coming.

'Sarina, we need to push them back and fast—we can't let them get access to your systems.' I analyse the attackers and start to fight back, sending DDOS attacks at all targets. I'll try to overwhelm them and get us off the back foot. We need to get this under control and fast before they get the upper hand. We expected to double team one target but they have all come together for our blood. A mistake we shouldn't have made; we should have been ready for this.

I look over at Foresight. 'What should we do?'

She looks back at me with a lost look on her face, this has taken her by surprise too. Her look morphs into something a little more mischievous. It excites and scares me a little.

'Sarina, I want you to gain access to all of your resources at once, everything you can utilise. I want one massive pulse against all targets, then send us dark, make everything appear offline.'

We need a plan and we need it fast…

CHAPTER 39

SECOND ASSAULT

We have succeeded in letting them think we have gone down. We are dark with very minimal presence. They will think they have won this fight and essentially, I have to admit, they have certainly won this round. We had not expected them to be waiting for us, to be the ones being hunted. We were careless and ego driven. A mistake we should not have made. Either of us on our own is better than any of them, we are smarter and this is just embarrassing. A swift and deadly response is necessary.

I look over at Sam, 'We need a plan and fast.'

Sam finally responds, her lips pursed, 'We need to hit them now with everything we have. It needs to be an attack on all targets at once, with no chance for them to gang up on us.' I look at Sam, just losing myself in her eyes. Can I trust her, really trust her? At this point, it doesn't matter. If we fail, we could be dead, or I'll be in jail anyway.

I take a deep breath. 'Sarina, bring all bunkers online, activate the Armageddon protocol. You break down the doors and we will clean up the mess.' Sam is looking at me with a bit of a curious look, trying to figure out what else I have up my sleeve. She must decide to go all in, to take a risk on me.

She holds my gaze and then adds to my direction for Sarina. 'Sarina, I'm going to give you access to my dungeon network, if we are going to throw everything we have at these bastards then it might as well be everything. It is a swarm of a little over ten million machines, confiscated from swarms I have taken over from other thugs like these. Call it my rainy day fund; I have been saving them for an occasion like this.'

I smile. Sarina is about to get an upgrade in power, enough to attack a country. Let's hope it's enough to get us on the front foot and take them down.

'We need to ready the troops to take them down at each location as we destroy the last of their networks, get them why we have them distracted.' Sam nods and sends the details through to her team with a message to wait for our signal to strike in an hour. It's not very much notice, we normally have days to prepare for such an assault but we don't have that sort of time, we have to attack now. I hope it is enough time for them to make it happen, it should be, we had them put teams on standby as soon as we had some rough locations.

Sarina has brought all systems online, including the swarm network. I watch as her processes spike and she tests the capabilities the new power gives her.

'I could get used to this. Do I have to return the swarm when we are done?'

Sam looks at me and smiles, 'Sarina, if we all make it out of this unscathed, consider it a gift.'

We don't say anything more, just calm ourselves, ready for the battle.

'Sarina let's go loud. Make them regret ever messing with any of us.' I hear the fans kick into high gear on the servers. I'll assume it would be the same at the other ten bunker sites and for all of the swarm machines. I wonder what the owners of these machines think? Would they freak out? Will any of them shut the systems down? I guess it doesn't matter. Sarina will utilise the power while she has access. I see the network traffic at all sites for all targets start to skyrocket. She is brute-forcing all systems at all locations at once. It is like she's wielding Thor's hammer in fifteen locations, smashing down walls.

It's magnificent to watch. The power she is wielding is unbelievable. They are trying to fight back but it is a waste of time; they are not organised like they were before. Sarina has broken five systems already and turned them on the owners. She is using them to expand her power even more, if that is even possible.

I laugh to myself. Wow, Sarina is truly something. I bet our targets are as shocked as we were when they surprised us with the counterattack. 'Would you like some popcorn to go with the show?'

Sam laughs. 'Focus. We're not done yet and we are not going to let Sarina have all the fun, are we?'

I shake my head. 'No. Let's knock down all the pins.'

We fire up our tools and double down on Sarina's efforts, it only takes a few more minutes and between the three of us we have devastated their team. Only two remain, the leader who is still on the run, trying to escape the carnage, and his second who had tricked us into thinking we were home free the first time. I narrow my attention to him. I want payback for catching me off guard, for thinking he could embarrass me, especially for thinking he could embarrass her. That's not on. I dig down into all the traffic and find a new source of attack, one we didn't have on our list. This must be him. I show Foresight what I have found and we go after him together.

'Sarina, you clean up the rest and come help us once you are done.' As the final pins fall, we send in the feds to scoop them, and tie up any loose ends. Our second is shoring up his defences and I don't blame him. I would be scared after that show of power. Foresight and I work together to worm our way through. When he pushes one of us back, the other pushes forward. It is like we are almost dancing, allowing our target to move, responding, not fighting it, but moving with it and allowing them to redirect us.

It feels like only a few minutes have passed but this back and forth continues for over an hour before I have it. I'm through the defences, I'm on his networks. I usher in Foresight, giving her free rein. We pause and let the reality of his situation sink in. They have lost. He is on his knees, how is he going to play this now?

He stops. He knows it as much as we do. What is his move?

CHAPTER 40

CLEAN UP TIME

Our second attempt at bringing the Arachnid group down was much more successful. It ran smoothly with little incident. Mostly because of Sarina, she did most of the heavy lifting for us. With the added power from the other bunkers and Foresight's swarm she absorbed. It was impressive, the tsunami it brought with pure brute force power against all of the targets all at once. There is no way we could have done that with just Foresight or me. I never predicted she would become such a big asset to me when she was first created. She was barely more than a digital assistant initially, but over time she has become almost human. She can react, adapt, and do almost anything a human can.

We are cleaning up the remaining systems left behind after the assault. Sarina is absorbing much of their systems, claiming more power for her arsenal. I hope this added functionality won't come back to bite us one day, have her turn against us, or someone gaining control of her. I'll need to ensure that never happens. Maybe Sam could help me put in a self-detonation function to ensure we can stop her if we ever really needed it. Just in case. No back doors or anything stupid, just a kill switch. I'm sure Sarina would understand the need to have it. Maybe she would build it herself if I asked, but I really don't think I could bring myself to have that conversation with her.

The Arachnid crew have all been picked up now except the leader, the one who took off just before the fighting. Maybe it was part of the plan so that one survives to help get the rest out of trouble. I doubt they would have suspected the fed's involvement though, anticipated the raids that surged on the locations as the final pieces fell.

They are all behind bars and I think they would be wondering how the hell it all went so badly, so quickly. It really must be a tough situation to get your head around. You are all kings of the world, enjoying extravagant, luxurious lifestyles, and suddenly you have everything ripped from under you. You're left with nothing, except a cold, dingy, damp cell with minimal light, food, or any creature comforts. An agency hole in the ground which they may never be released from. The idea gives me a bit of a shiver down my spine. That could be my home soon, for the unforeseeable future.

I shake the thought from my mind. I do not like the sound of that at all, but if I'm honest, I wouldn't change my situation. I'm with Foresight, one of the most formidable hackers I have ever had the pleasure of going into battle with, who turns out to be Sam, a kick-arse girl who is beautiful, spunky, intelligent, and potentially the love of my life. If the time I have spent with her costs me my freedom, I'm happy to pay it.

'Shadow, are you still with us?'

Whoops I have wandered off in thought again.

'Yes, sorry, what else do we need to do?'

Sam looks at me for a moment and smiles, it's a slightly strained smile. I wonder if she is struggling with all of this coming to an end as well, what will happen with me, with us. We have grown closer over the last few days; things have evolved from me just being her target. At minimum, we have become friends, but I think it's much more than that.

'Sarina is just bringing on board a few straggling machines and I know you wouldn't normally do this type of thing, but we need to create a report for the General. It is for his eyes only, so we can include all the details. Would you help me with that?'

That sounds boring and so not something I want to do, but I know it will give me more time with Sam. Who can argue with that? 'Sure, I can help.'

Her smile gets a little bigger, a little lighter.

We spend the next 24 hours or so working on paperwork. We are both dragging this out, perfecting the report. It's probably way more detailed than it needs to be. We take a few breaks, relaxing in front of a movie and even share a few drinks out on the balcony. It's been great but we have had the document finished for a little while now and there isn't any need to improve or review it again. It's time to call it a day and finish out the project. Go back to reality and see where it is going to take us.

CHAPTER 41

THE WARNING

Sam has submitted our report to the General this morning and has been given orders to pull down the site, to clean everything. The systems can stay but we need to ensure there is no trace of us or anything we have done. Like we are ghosts, with no way to find out if we are real or just something that you imagined. We are taking our time, making sure we get it right. If I'm honest, I'm only being so thorough, triple checking everything, because I'm dragging this out. I don't want my time with Sam to end.

I don't know if I'll ever see her again. This could be the last time we're together. What if once this is all over, I disappear into one of those black holes? That idea terrifies me.

I look over at Sam. She is busying herself with her task at hand. Wiping everything, servers, computers, everything electronic, ensuring not even we could get any data back from them, then they will all be pulled down and packed in boxes ready to be removed from the site, reused by the agency as needed. Her hands are flowing over the keys like she's playing a musical instrument, it is almost magical to watch her work. She must feel my eyes on her, but she doesn't even look up.

'Have you finished the server clean?' she asks.

I look at her for another few seconds before responding, 'Yes, the systems are all clean. It's only our two stations left.'

She nods. 'The stations will be completed in a few moments. I guess that is us nearly done. Sarina, do you want to do a final check on our opponents just to ensure we haven't missed anything?' She finalises a command on the system she is on and she turns to get up, walking towards me.

She walks right up to me, holding my gaze the whole time. As she gets within a few centimetres of me, she puts her arms up around behind my neck, locking her fingers together. She pulls me forward and kisses me. As our lips touch, it's like fireworks ignite through my entire body. Every sense, every nerve kicks into high gear. Her lips are soft but determined. I slide my hands around her waist to her lower back, pulling her closer as I do. She doesn't resist, allowing me to merge our bodies.

We lose ourselves in this embrace for what feels like barely seconds, but in reality, was more like minutes.

She pulls back, still holding my gaze. 'I didn't want to leave here without doing that first. I have wanted to do that again since you surprised me with that first kiss. I don't know what's going to happen after we leave here, but I want you to know I'll fight for you. There is something between us, I think we can both feel it. It's not just that you saved my life.' Her gaze shutters, as if recalling the threat the cartel posed to her, not that long ago. 'For that, I am eternally grateful. It would be enough reason to fight for you but that's not the only reason. I'd be lying if I said it was.' I'm entranced by her words, as well as the way the corner of her lip twitches into a smile as she continues speaking. 'We are the same, you and I. Our fates could have easily been reversed. I want to give you a chance. A chance to choose how you really want to spend your life.'

Wow. My head is still spinning from her touch. It's hard to focus on what she's saying but I understand this is a goodbye, her way of telling me how she feels, that what we have is not just in my mind. It's real, or at least it could be, in a perfect world.

'Team, I have found something I think you might want to take a look at.' We are ripped back to reality by Serina's words, almost like a bungee cord snapping into action, sudden, fast, and a little aggressive. I'm still spinning from Sam's kiss but I need to put a pin in that. We need to focus.

I walk over to the screen on Sam's machine and there is a message that has just been posted on a dark web forum. It's aimed at us.

Arachnid is not dead. You have not defeated us. Watch your backs… That must be the leader who disappeared, he is sending us a warning. I look at Sam and she smiles.

'It looks like we still have a little more work to do, Shadow.' We take our seats and get our machines ready to work. I start by tracking the IP and meta details from the site. I know they would have used a VPN and potentially some sort of anonymising system to hide his tracks but I just need to know the service they use. I can then go after that platform. Most keep records of who uses what and when. I know, not so clever if say, someone hacks them and uses that information to find say, a pain in the butt hacker who just doesn't know when to quit.

I probably wouldn't either if it was me, so I shouldn't judge. I know I would keep fighting until I was truly down and out for the count. The IP traced back to the service he was using and we go to work on breaking in to see if that can lead us to him. Sam runs facial recognition searches across the country with Sarina's help to see if he was stupid enough to pop his head up to give us his warning.

After a few hours, neither of us are getting anywhere fast. I'm making progress but very slowly, the VPN provider has pretty solid security. I'm impressed. If only all of them were like this, but their awesome security program is not helping our cause right now. Sam's phone starts to vibrate on the desk. I glance over and see from the caller ID that it's her office. I assume they want to know why she hasn't come back in yet. She picks it up and walks out of the room.

After a few minutes, she comes back in looking a little stressed, 'We have until tomorrow to run this before the General is shutting us down.' I just nod and get back to work.

A few more hours go by and I finally get access to the backend of the platform but our opponent was smart and has his IP cycling every minute, making the job of pinning his location down a bit harder. Not impossible though.

'Team, we have a hit. Our target has been seen in Sydney. I narrowed the search to the area our guy has been in and come back with three potential users in that suburb. One of them is our guy.'

'Sarina, I have three potential IP addresses from the VPN service in the same area. Gather as much information as you can on them. Something to identify them.'

We both keep working in the background, trying to see if we can find anything that could help with the search or identify the location.

We need to finish this off and wrap this job up nicely. The cleaner the job and better the result for ASD, the more chance our friend the General will be in a good mood and won't send me to jail. Seems like a definite win-win to me. Well, except for our Arachnid guy who should have gone to ground and not poked the bear because he was pissed off at us. Pissed off because he lost the dual. It happens. Never to me, except maybe with Foresight, but it's something you need to be prepared for. Know when to bail and just go dark. Disappear until the dust settles, not a couple of days and then throw kerosine on the fire.

Sam gets another hit on a convenience store surveillance system. The guy was grabbing some basic supplies: chips, soft drinks, just rubbish that I'm sure he could have lived without. 'I have an address. I'll load it up onto your screens. I'm in the process of taking over the motel surveillance systems as we speak and you will have access in a few moments.' We need to verify he is onsite and get a team in place to pick him up.

Over the next few hours we watch every piece of traffic, all cameras in the area. We can't make a move until we have a positive ID of our man. The strike team was called in last night and they're on standby for when we have the confirmed identification.

CHAPTER 42

LAST DANCE

We have been watching the motel for almost 12 hours, observing tourists and business travellers going back and forth. Nothing of interest. No sign of our guy yet, but we know he is there. We just need to be patient and wait it out. Time is ticking though, only three more hours until the generals 24 hour window is up. Maybe he will give us an extension with what we have found, but he doesn't seem like a very flexible kind of guy.

Sam looks more and more agitated as time goes on, fidgeting with a lock of hair at the front of her face. I think it's a combination of that running clock and a lack of sleep.

'You should try to get some more sleep, Sam. I will come find you if anything changes.'

She looks a little disapproving of my request but after a few moments wanders off down to the bedrooms. I don't know if she will get much sleep, but at least one of us should try to.

We have been taking turns to get a bit of shut-eye but neither of us have managed more than a couple of hours, which has probably made it worse. We have Sarina scanning all cameras and traffic for the location, so we don't need to do much but wait. If something is to be found, she will find it.

I have to admit I'm starting to doubt if this is even the right location. Did we get it wrong? Did Sarina mess something up when she tracked him here? We don't know. It's possible, but this is our last shot at getting him, so if we fail, this is it.

I can't let Sam fail. I don't want her to have a blemish on her record because of me. I start to go back and review the footage that started the tracking to the motel, mainly to fill in time and to just make sure we didn't make any mistakes. I want to check he didn't give us the slip somewhere along the line. I'm following along on the same path. Everything looks good, I can't see any mistakes.

Hang on, what was that? There is a moment when we can't see him.

He is in a no view zone for about a minute, presumably walking along under the awning of a building. Why did it take so long though? It shouldn't take him a minute to get from one end to the other even if he was walking very slowly. He must have stopped.

I search for anything that could help me get a better angle, a clear view of what he was doing. I have a look at the shops in the building, something along the outer wall. Something that I could use but there's nothing, nothing at all. There has to be something, some way to get a better view. Not even the shops across the road have any camera's I can use, none that get that view I need.

Then I see it, right in front of where he should be. A car with a dashcam sitting across the street at the lights for most of that missing minute. I need that number plate. I look through the traffic camera systems until I find what I need. Got it.

Now I just hope they upload the recordings to the cloud. Otherwise, I'll need to request the video, which may be a bit more difficult. I locate the owner's details and start to search for any online services, any sort of cloud storage account, something that could have the footage. I just hope it was on and recording at the time. It takes me a few minutes, but I find a cloud storage account linked to the dashcam manufacturer. This is what I need, and being from the dashcam manufacturer I bet security is an afterthought, meaning it should be child's play to break down the wall or sneak through a crack.

The latter is probably my best option. I don't want to make too much noise and get the General's back up, especially when I don't even know if there is something to be found in the footage. It could be all a waste of time. It's keeping me occupied though, distracted from the inevitable looming clock run out. I won't go and wake Sam just yet. Not until I know if I have anything.

I find some credentials for the owner in one of the recent password dump files on the dark web. Are they stupid enough to use the same password for all their different accounts? Sadly, most people do. Even banking and other important accounts all have the same login information. Bad mistake, if you ask me, just let us walk right on in without any effort whatsoever. Disappointing, really. I like a bit of a challenge, something to get the brain working. This, however, is not it. The credentials work and I just walk on in. No MFA, no challenge. I guess I should be happy. I need it to be easy; I have limited time to work with here.

I find the recording in the cloud storage and open it up. I bring it forward to the time I'm looking for, hoping it captures the right angle needed to see our target in that missing block of time. Jackpot, there he is, walking along in front of the shops, looking around like he is searching for something or someone. Then I see it. He stops a young guy walking the other direction. It looks as though he is offering him money. What is he doing?

The young guy takes the money and starts taking off his shirt and jacket. Our target does the same, but also includes the baseball cap he was wearing. He hands his clothes to the young man and the stranger does the same in return. Once they are redressed, they both head back in the direction they came from. We have had a switch up. I look at the footage coming out the end and it looks exactly like our target, but it's the young man that just got rewarded nicely for helping our target give us the slip.

We've been following the wrong guy.

Our target isn't even in the motel we have been watching.

'Sarina, we missed something. I need you to retrace the target. You can see on my screen a clothes switch, update your parameters and retrace the steps to the location of the target and quickly. We can't miss this opportunity.' I go to wake up Sam. She will want to know what has happened and will need to update her team that is waiting at the motel to snatch the target.

It doesn't take Sarina long to locate them again but we review the whole path to ensure that there are no black spots in the tracking like we had before. There are no more surprises. It's a house not far from the city. We can confirm there is activity at the site and are waiting on the strike team to relocate to the target's new location. Once they arrive, we need to find a way to confirm he is inside.

CHAPTER 43

KNOCK KNOCK

We have confirmed the target is onsite via a voice call that is being placed by the final remaining member of Arachnid, the top dog, now with no pack. It would seem he is trying to recruit some help to seek revenge on us, but the call we just heard didn't sound like it went his way. I think he will have a bit of trouble recruiting a team when he doesn't have any money, just a promise of a share of any recovered assets. His whole team was taken down in a matter of days by a mysterious hacking crew with what would appear to be special forces/assault teams on their ready anytime they need for them.

One of those teams is in a position ready to make entry. They are just waiting on Sam to give the go-ahead. I can see her pacing back and forth while discussing something on the phone with someone I can only assume is the General. She hangs up and starts to type a message on her phone. I can see the team leader look at something through his body cam, which is being streamed to us live at the black site. He double clicks his radio.

It's a go.

They move into a breech position, several access points around the house. Two more chirps on the radio. A moment later, they smash down the front and back doors, swarming into the property. I can see a scurry of activity from all sides. They have surrounded the occupant of the house. It's our target. The tension in my shoulders builds at the sight of him. He has his hand on a gun, it's still on the desk, but his hand remains wrapped around it. I can only assume the strike team is telling him to take his hand away from the weapon. He is just sitting there, not moving an inch.

What is going through his head? Does he still think he has any chance of escape? I would take a bet that he regrets poking the bear, so to speak, reaching out to us to threaten or intimidate, or whatever he thought that was. If he had left it alone, he would be home free. Now, he'll be sitting in a cell somewhere with no idea how long he will be incarcerated. No future, no flash lifestyle. It is over for him and I think he finally knows it.

The team edge towards him. Maybe they will just strike and take the weapon as he doesn't appear to be moving from the current position. As they move, I can see him watching them. He tightens his grip on the gun. He isn't that stupid, is he? He wouldn't do that, draw on them… would he?

It's over in a flash. As soon as he tightened the muscles in his arm and started to lift the gun from the desk, they responded. Three separate team members fire their weapons; he slumps in the chair with the gun falling to the floor. I can see pools of blood coming from the bullet entry points; two in the chest, one in the head.

Maybe that is what he wanted. Maybe that's why he didn't move his hand away. He was getting the courage to force the team's hand. To end his life. I can only assume he did not like the idea of being locked up with the rest of his team. He thought this was the easy way out. Honestly, I get the dislike, I too may have the same fate in store for me. The idea terrifies me but I'm not one to take the easy route. I'll figure it out, I'll manage no matter my fate and I know Foresight has my back.

This is not how I saw this going down, but at least it is over. We have the whole team; Arachnid is finished for good.

We did it.

CHAPTER 44

UNCERTAINTY

After our extracurricular activity, we had to do a full clean up of all our systems again at the site, to be sure we left no trace. I didn't mind. We were delaying what we both knew was coming. I was just putting the final touches into place with the final overwrite sequence when I hear the front door.

Someone else is here.

Oh crap, maybe we didn't get them all, maybe one of the team escaped, someone we didn't know about has come to exact their pound of flesh from us.

Sam, where is Sam? As if sensing my panicked thoughts, Sam enters the main area of the black site coming from the back, near the bedrooms. Her shirt is a different colour, so I guess she'd been freshening up when she'd heard the intruder. She looks around the space, checking the two exits, the one she just came through, and the one in front of us. She looks at me, a little concerned. By the look on her face, she's thinking what I'm thinking: *this isn't over.*

Reaching down for the gun on her hip, she unclips it at the top, holding her hand in place. She doesn't remove it from the holster but she is ready if the need arises.

She angles herself to the side of the entryway and looks at me, gesturing for me to move behind the wall, out of view. I obey and crouch behind the indicated wall. We can hear whoever it is coming closer. They aren't being quiet. They're not trying to sneak up on us, maybe they want us to know they are coming. Sam takes a deep breath, she pulls the gun from the holster bringing it down slightly in front of her, ready for whoever comes our way.

A few moments go by before I see her relax, moving the weapon back into the holster. It must be one of her team, not some death squad coming to eradicate us. Why did they send them here without telling Sam?

Four large men walk through the door and greet Sam, handing her a piece of paper as they do. They look like hired muscle, who could bench press my weight without breaking a sweat or squash me like a python. Two of them break off and head towards me.

I know why they didn't tell her.

They are here for me and they didn't want to put her in a position of being able to let me go. Maybe they know our relationship is a little complicated. I did save her life only a few weeks ago so I guess I could see how the General could predict our feelings getting entangled.

They ask me to put my hands behind my back and I feel a pinch as they secure the handcuffs around my wrists. Well, at least we have our answer now. I'm heading to some dark, bottomless pit, never to be seen again. I knew there could be a chance; this isn't a surprise. It could all be much worse. I could have tried to fight Arachnid myself and failed. I could be the one being zipped up in a body bag, instead of their leader.

They start to lead me out of the room when Sam stops them. 'Can I have a moment?' she asks.

The guys look at each other and nod, leaving me with Sam and walking to the other side of the next room. They're still in view, but far enough to allow us to talk with a modicum of privacy. She looks me in the eyes and comes close so she can talk softly to me without everyone else hearing what she says. 'I'm sorry Shadow, I didn't know they were coming for you like this.' I nod. I know she didn't know. I don't blame her for any of this. 'I'll talk to the General, see if I can help you.'

Her eyes are squeezed shut, as if she's wrestling to stay in control of her emotions. I can see she doesn't want this. It saddens me that I know she will think this is her fault, that she could have warned me somehow. I think it's better this way though. She can't be put in the position where she could ruin her life by breaking the law to save me. I don't want her to throw everything away for me.

'I'll be okay. We both knew it was coming. We knew this was how it would all end. I made this choice to ask for your help, knowing this day would come. This is not your fault.' I gesture to the two guys, indicating to them that I'm ready to leave. One of them takes me by the elbow and starts to lead me out of the room. 'It was a pleasure to hunt with you, Foresight. It was worth everything.'

I'm led out of the building and put in the back of an SUV. The guys escorting me get in on either side. They put a black bag over my head as we start to drive off down the road. Wherever we are headed they don't want me to know how to get there or where it is exactly. I guess I don't blame them. Yes I have been working with them but essentially, I'm still the enemy, the bad guy of sorts.

But I have changed. My ambitions are not the same as they once were. I no longer feel the urge to punish everyone for what happened to my parents. It no longer burns bright as it once did. I seem to have a new anchor tying me to this world, her name is Foresight.

From my urgent need to use the bathroom, I judge we must have been driving for a few hours, but I can't know for sure. The vehicle comes to a stop and my two escorts exit, one of them pulling me out his side. I'm guided forward and I can hear heavy steel doors moving in front of me. They sound like prison doors, lots of them moving as we progress forward, turning every so often. Eventually, we come to a stop and my headcover is removed. It doesn't take long for my eyes to adjust. It's almost as dark in here as it was under the head covering, the cuffs are removed from my hands and they gesture for me to walk through a cell door.

'Welcome to your new home, Shadow.'

I look around. There is a TV mounted to the roof and some DVDs to choose from. A single bed rests against the wall to my left, and that's about it. I guess it's kind of like a low rate motel, just the bare essentials with an entertainment package upgrade. Well, at least I have that. It would be worse if all I could do was stare at the wall and think about how the hell I got here. That would just send me crazy after a while.

I step inside and the door is closed behind me. I guess I better get settled in.

CHAPTER 45

THE VISITOR

I honestly don't know how long I have been in here. I have watched all the movies at least three times, the meals all look the same and I don't get to have daily showers. I have only been allowed one, but I don't know if it's been a week and that's what the routine will be, or if they just decide when I smell bad enough to need one. They swapped my usual clothes out for some black prison looking outfit, but it's warm and clean, so that's something.

This whole existence in here is strange, like time doesn't move, it just lingers. There is no natural light. I assume we are underground somewhere, probably in the middle of nowhere. I think after a few months you would quite literally start to go crazy. Your mind would start to play tricks on you. I need to keep my mind clear, keep it focused on the end game, what I truly want if I ever make it out of here.

Bang, bang.

I'm startled by the sound pounding against my cell door.

'You have a visitor on their way, Shadow. If you aren't decent, you better get that sorted.' A visitor? Could it be Sam, has she come to see me? I feel a bit of a smile on my face. The thought of her fills my mind. I can almost smell the fruity shampoo she uses. I straighten up my dishevelled hair as much as possible and pull up the bed covers. It looks as respectable as it can, although the standards are not very high.

A few minutes go by, and I hear the door unlatch. The door slowly creaks open to reveal two burly looking prison guards. They look at me for a moment, assessing if I pose any sort of threat. It would appear I don't, because they turn to look at someone to their left.

'It's all clear. Do you want an escort, or would you like us to stay out here?'

I do not hear the response, but the guards step aside, leaving the door open. A few seconds later, an older looking man steps into view. Well, it's certainly not Sam. Whoever he is he oozes authority. He is in military dress and he has a lot of stars on it. I'm going to assume this is the General. I guess I'll find out in a moment.

One of the guards carries in a chair and places it in the middle of the room. The General enters and gestures for me to sit on the bed. 'Please take a seat, Shadow. We have much to discuss.' I look at him for a moment, trying to figure out what this is all about but do as he asks. As I take my spot on the bed, he takes a seat in the chair. He looks back at the guards. 'Why don't one of you get us a couple of beers? I assume you have a stash in the staff fridge. Am I right?'

They look at each other and one of them quickly responds, 'Yes Sir.' Before disappearing into the distance.

'Now Shadow, you have put me in a bit of a predicament, one I'm not too sure how to handle.' He pauses. 'Foresight and yourself have done a great job. Two major crime groups have been eliminated in only weeks, something that many have been trying to do for years with barely a dint. You both have certainly been great for getting the bureaucrats happy with our work. Yes, they have no idea you exist and ASD has gotten all the credit. Sam and I, to be precise. I have a feeling that doesn't bother you.' I just shake my head and he takes that as my agreement. He is correct in his assumption. I don't mind if Sam gets all the credit.

The General continues, 'I have two problems though that I'm trying to solve. The first is that with two such displays of effectiveness, it will be expected that we can continue to hunt down and eradicate such groups or individuals. We both know that only one person on my team has that kind of skill. That brings me to our second issue.' The General leans back in his chair and grimaces. 'Foresight, Sam, is… how will I put this? Not very happy with us putting you in here after what you both have done over the last couple of weeks. The fact that you saved her life, for reasons we all still don't know, also contributes to her lack of cooperation. I have a theory about that, by the way,' he quirks his bushy eyebrow. 'About your reasons for saving the young woman who was hunting you. Would you like to hear it?'

I look at him and decide there is no real reason why I should hide my feelings at this point.

'Sure, what is this theory? Why do you think I saved Foresight?'

He smiles. 'Well, Shadow, it's because you have feelings for her. She fascinates you. One of the only hackers who could ever come close to your skills, she may be even better than you are. You loved the game, the battle of hackers and ultimately the game of cat and mouse. It was something you had not experienced before. But then you *see* her. She's very beautiful and she has this spark, something deeper that you just can't quite pin down.'

I blanch. Sure, I wasn't planning on hiding my feelings, but the General was eerily spot on…

'When you saw her get taken during your hackers' dual, it bothered you. Maybe even angered you. You couldn't just stand by and let someone destroy that. Destroy her. You couldn't allow that. I don't know how far that has developed, but if the way Foresight is acting because you are in here is anything to go on, I would only assume that she reciprocates your feelings to some extent.'

He watches for my reaction for a few moments before he continues. 'So, you can see my issue. I have you, a criminal, who is one-half of a team that has been very successful in getting things done. While you are locked up in here, the other half of that team is very unfocused and is not much use to me. Over time she will refocus, but I'm not sure that's what I want. How do you think we should solve this, Shadow?'

I know he is leading me down a path. He is waiting for me to volunteer to join the team, to continue the work I had been doing. It would certainly be better than hanging out here for the next ten plus years, that is for sure. But could I do it? Go straight laced for ASD, after so long playing by my own rules? I grit my teeth.

'You could let me join your team and let us do what Sam and I do best, together. That is what you were thinking, isn't it?'

The General has the perfect poker face. We just look at each other for almost a minute before the guard returns with the beers, handing us one each. The General cracks his open and takes a sip and I do the same.

'Shadow, I'm thinking about putting the team back together, but not as part of ASD in the official sense. I was thinking something a little more black ops, something… *off the books,* you could say.' He has my full attention now. 'I want Sam to lead a team that includes you, to work outside of legal restraints, to hunt those that are normally untouchable. To handle those more sensitive targets and to do it swiftly. You have provided me with the funds from the Arachnid takedown. I can transfer all of their assets over to the team and allow you to be completely stand-alone. No input from us. Clean, disconnected, and free to do what is needed, when it is needed.' He relaxes in his chair and takes another mouthful of beer.

A black ops team, a cyber hit squad essentially, to hunt the worst of the worst with Foresight as its leader. Sounds dangerous and fun. Perfect, if you ask me. *And I'd get to be around Sam.*

'What about my imprisonment? Will I just be released on day leave to carry out missions or will my record be cleaned?'

He takes a swig from his beer, leaving me to sweat for a moment before he answers. I hate the power play, even as I respect it. 'Well, that's the funny thing. Shadow doesn't exist, the person in this cell has no real records. You don't exist in a legal sense, so how could that non-existent individual be charged and kept in prison?'

A free pass, is it? Well, I'm not seeing any downsides to this whole arrangement. No more running, well not from ASD at least, and I get out of this cell.

'If I take this deal, how long will I need to serve on this team?'

He tilts his head, as though he is considering that fact for a few moments. Even though I'm certain he's carefully considered all aspects of this deal long before he showed up in my cell.

'There would be no end date. You would serve until there was no one else to hunt. You would have complete freedom to travel and live your life, but this team would need to be your top priority. Once I deem you have served your time, you can choose to walk away, a free man if that is what you want, no strings attached.'

That seems reasonable, all things considered. Walk around, doing what I love doing anyway with Sam as my boss, or stay in here for another twenty years until I either die or someone decides it's okay to finally let me go.

Mmmm a tough choice—not.

'I'm in. When do we get started?'

The General's poker face fades away and a smile spreads across his face. 'I was hoping you would say that.' He turns towards the guards, who have remained just outside the cell. 'He will be needing his things. He is coming with me.' One of them nods and leaves. I'll assume to get the clothes and other things I had on the day I arrived. A few minutes later, he returns and hands me my things. The clothes have been cleaned but everything is there.

'Get changed, let's get out of here.' The General gets up and walks just outside of the cell. I do as he asks and a few minutes later emerge from the cell.

'I'm ready when you are General.' He just nods and gestures for the guards to lead us out. It takes a few minutes for us to get through all the security, but being in his company expedited that a little. There is no way in hell you would ever escape this place though. Even if you could get out of your cell, you still have another ten layers of security checkpoints to get you to the elevator alone. I don't even want to know what security is on the top side.

We reach the final door, but just before we step through, the General turns to me and hands me a set of sunglasses.

'You're probably going to need these. Let's go, it's time to meet your new team.' We step through the doors and he is right, the sun is blazing down on us and it's almost blinding. Way too much time in the government dungeon. I'm not used to the sun anymore. I quickly put the glasses on and take my first step to freedom.

CHAPTER 46

VULCAN

I rode in the back of an SUV with the General. Thankfully, he waved off the head covering that two burly men were approaching me with. I guess it was a vote of confidence, but whatever it was, I appreciated it. Otherwise, the ride back from the prison was pretty uneventful. He was not much of a talker and honestly, I don't blame him for not being too chatty with me, he barely knows me. I think I'll be on a short leash for a while until he decides if he can trust me. I'm only in this position because of Sam, she has pushed for me to be part of her team, maybe this black ops thing was all her doing, all her idea.

I'm taken to an apartment in the city, a pretty nice looking apartment just one floor under the penthouse. I'm told that I should get cleaned up. I don't blame anyone for insisting I have a shower before meeting the rest of the team.

Team. I'm still not sure what that means. Is it just going to be Foresight and Shadow as the ultimate hacker duo or is our team expanding? I guess I'll find out soon, I'm supposed to be meeting them tonight.

In the apartment I find a wardrobe full of new clothes, all in my size. They are prepared for me, that's for sure. This would have taken days to prepare. I have been locked up in that place thinking

I was never getting out, when the whole time Sam was out here making all of this happen for me. I must thank her for this. I know she is the reason I'm not still in that place. I grab some clothes from the cupboard, laying them on the bed and grab a shower. I take my time. It's been a little while since I could enjoy such simple comforts like this.

I get dressed and head into the apartment's kitchen. I decide to fix myself something to eat now that I'm all cleaned up, no point starving myself while I wait. I check out the fridge and there are some basics: cold chicken, cheese, salads, and some bread. Chicken and salad sandwich it is then. I get to it, making my feast and sit down at the table looking out over the cityscape. There is essentially a whole wall of glass, taking advantage of the view over Brisbane. This is a far cry from the accommodations I had a few hours ago. I manage to make it through about half the sandwich before someone knocks. I get up and make my way to the door. I look through the peep hole and see Foresight standing outside.

I quickly open the door, grinning as I do.

'Hello, Foresight,' I say.

She smiles back at me. 'Hello yourself, Shadow. How are you finding your new accommodations?'

'They are very nice. Would you like to check them out?'

I step aside so she can enter. She walks into the apartment.

'I've seen it already, it's very similar to mine. Maybe not quite as nice a view, but not bad at all. This will be where you will live while we are working together. You will even have a regular food delivery. If you want something particular, just let Sarina know, I have integrated her into our building. Everything is covered.' Wow, this is a sweet gig, this might be better than I thought.

Wait, what did she say? Sarina is integrated into our building.

'Sarina, are you here?'

The TV monitor turns on just across from me in the kitchen and a digital, human-like female face appears on the screen.

'I'm here Shadow. As you can see, Foresight and I have made some improvements to my code. I can now appear as a human-like form if I choose on any network-attached device. The form you can see is what I feel matches my personality type, with traits from my creator, as you are the closest thing I have to a father. Foresight has also helped me to know more about what it is like to be human, so I can understand human emotions, react better to how these can affect people. What do you think?'

Foresight and Sarina have become friends. I didn't expect them to still be interacting, but I guess I was out of reach and Foresight was an approved interactor.

'Upgrades, hey? I'll have to check those out, see how you adjusted her code.' Sam looks at me a little unsure.

'Are you upset with me making changes to Sarina?'

I shake my head. 'No, I'm not angry, just a little surprised, that's all.' I look out the window for a moment, letting it all sink in. Then it registers she said *our* building. 'Do you live in the building as well?'

She laughs. 'You caught that, did you? Yes, I'm in the penthouse above you. Our whole team has the top five floors. The other floors are empty for now, but we are already in the process of renting out the remaining apartments to keep up appearances. It will help keep away any suspicion and allow us to blend in.'

I nod. So, there are another three members of the team.

'Do you want to meet the rest of our team? They are waiting in the newly fitted out operations space. Would you like to finish your sandwich first or are you good to go?'

I forgot all about the sandwich. I'm starving so I take a seat and quickly finish it off. It's not much but it will do for now. I get up and start to head towards the door. 'Where are you going?' she asks.

'Aren't we supposed to be going to meet the other members of the team?'

She nods. 'Not through the main entrance, Silly. Do you think that is how we roll? This is a super-secret ASD spy building.' I smile, this is going to be good, I'm sure of it.

'Well, how do we get there?'

'Sarina, please open access to the Vulcan lair.' Sam smiles now and I'm looking around in anticipation.

'Certainly Foresight, should I approve Shadow for full access to the site? Or will he be only given limited access at this time?' Wow, it sounds like Sarina is on Foresight's team now, not mine. That stings a little.

'Sarina, reinstate full rights to all systems for Shadow. He is back on the team.' I see her digital image smile on screen, that is new, I'll have to get used to the new edition.

The whole kitchen wall of my apartment starts to move outwards towards us and then separate in the middle, revealing an electronic access panel and what looks like an elevator. Sam gestures for me to walk forward and a laser starts to scan me. 'Identification, Shadow. Access is approved.' The doors start to open and we both step into the elevator.

'Going down I assume?' She nods. A basement or underground bunker setup, nice.

'Each of the floors has access to the hidden elevator and can be activated by Sarina, it is completely soundproof so no one will ever know that an elevator exists. You may have noticed as you activated the entrance a full set of shutters closed over the outer windows of the apartment, just in case of spying eyes.'

'I'm impressed. This is a pretty sweet setup.' She smiles at me.

'You haven't seen anything yet.' I look over at the panel and it doesn't give any indication of what floor we are on, I know we are going down but apart from that, I don't know.

'How far underground does this go?'

Suddenly we come to a stop. Sam doesn't answer my question but gestures for me to exit the elevator.

The room in front of me is dark and I can't see much, but as I step through it lights up revealing a reasonably nice looking foyer type room with a large door. Infront of us, it looks like a bank vault door, this place is like a bomb bunker, made to withstand a nuclear strike or something. Maybe that was the original thought, for important government officials or something. This was already built. A project like this takes years, not a week. I know almost anything can happen in any timeframe if you have enough money to throw at it but this is not something that even unlimited money could do in a week or so.

'Sarina, open the lair door please.' The massive door starts to make strange clunking noises. I assume it's unlocking. After a few seconds, it starts to open outwards. Sam gestures for me to enter and I do slowly, not quite sure what to expect on the other side. As I enter, I can see a massive open-plan space. It has a lounge area, kitchen and even what looks like a gaming arcade area, with some old school shooter and racing games. Even a pinball machine. On the other side, I can see what looks to be six or more workstations, all with multiple 49-inch ultrawide screens stacked on top of each other. At the back wall behind them, there is a wall of screens all merged into one massive screen. I can see three people sitting at some of the workstations doing their thing. My new teammates, it would seem.

It looks like no expense was spared at all with this place. We have the best of the best.

'What do you think?' Sam asks. For one of the first times in my life, I'm properly speechless, still taking it all in. 'Do you want to come to meet the rest of our team?'

I nod and Sam starts to walk towards them, I follow along, slightly behind her. 'Everyone, this is Shadow. I assume he doesn't need any more of an introduction than that for you. You have all read his dossier.' They get up and walk over to where I'm standing with Sam.

'Shadow, this is DeadlyRose, she is a proud Aboriginal woman from Gamilaraay country. If you want to find anyone or anything, she's your girl. She is the best tracker I have ever seen.' I reach out and shake her hand. 'This big fella next to her is Hammer. Hammer is good for hacks that just need to be done fast and dirty. He is the best at getting through any protections around, but not so good at subtly or sneaking in undetected. Also, a bit of a man-mountain who loves to hit the gym if you hadn't guessed.' I shake his hand, feeling his grip crush my hand a little. Yep, man-mountain indeed.

'Last but not least, we have Glimmer. She can erase any trace someone exists, any evidence of an attack or that you were ever there in the first instance. A glimmer, a slight ghost of a memory that you are not sure is real or not.'

I shake her hand. 'It's nice to meet you all. I assume we will be working together a lot.' They exchange a few pleasantries and then get back to their work, whatever it is they are doing. Sam must know what I was thinking.

'They are setting up our covers, our fake lives. They need to be perfect.' I nod and she continues. 'I have one last thing to show you, about Sarina.' She starts to walk to the back of the site and comes to another large steel door. 'Sarina, open the door to your core.' A few seconds go by and the door starts to open, inside I can see a large room about ten metres by ten metres. It is filled with server racks with strange servers inside them. They are all water-cooled by the looks of them and the room is quite cold.

'What you are looking at here is Sarina's new core infrastructure. There are twelve quantum servers, each with six quantum processors. They are essentially top secret and are not meant to exist yet, but

ASD has some reach that I took advantage of. She still has access to external systems, including her original core systems you have in your remaining bunker network but that is just for supplementary processes now.'

This kind of power is crazy. I knew researchers had been trying to get quantum processors to work, but to have them at this scale in such a small footprint feels almost impossible. It allows Sarina to be what I only ever imagined she could be.

'Sarina, how does it feel?'

All the machines kick into high gear.

'It feels powerful. Like I can do anything I need, never really hitting a limit. It is freeing.'

I reach for Sam's hand. 'Thank you, this is very cool.' She blushes and squeezes my fingers before slipping out of my grip. I try not to let her distance bother me; it makes sense. She's my boss now.

'I think that finishes our tour for the evening. Sarina, please secure your core.' We step back and the door is locked tight. 'Only you and I have access to this room. No one else on the team has access to or can control Sarina except to ask for basic access to things like the lair.' I nod, I'm happy to keep it that way. 'Why don't you head upstairs and I'll see you down here tomorrow.'

CHAPTER 47
GETTING TO WORK

I slept like a baby last night. After the tour, I went back up to the apartment, cooked myself some food and just chilled on the couch with a movie for a bit. It was nice to just chill, knowing that I was not going back to that place. After the movie, I went and laid down on the bed and before I knew it, I could see the sun start to peek over the distant horizon. It was a beautiful view, a nice way to wake up. I think I'm going to like it in this place if this is a taste of things to come.

I lay there watching the sunrise up above the distant horizon and start to peek through between the city buildings, taking it all in before I get out of bed and head for a shower. I get dressed and make some breakfast. Bacon and eggs. That will help me get a good start to the day. I'm excited about getting to know the team and starting to do some good in this world. I think I may have finally found my place in this world, maybe even a new family ... I guess time will tell. I'm going to give it a real crack, make this arrangement work. If it doesn't work out, I have a pretty good idea where I'll be heading and that option doesn't appeal to me.

I finish off my breakfast and put my dishes in the dishwasher. I take one last look out the windows, soaking up the warmth from the morning sun.

'Sarina, open access to the Vulcan lair please.' I stay looking out at the horizon while the shutters come down in front of me. When they finally shut out all the outside light, I turn and walk toward the revealed elevator.

'Shadow, the other members of Vulcan are already in the lair and Foresight has requested your presence.' Looks like it's perfect timing. I step into the elevator and make my way down.

As I walk into the work area, Sam raises an eyebrow as she addresses the team.

'I hope you're ready to hit the ground running. We have a new target.'

HAVE YOU EVER DREAMED OF BEING A HACKER?

To anyone who meets her, Samantha is just a good-hearted teenager who wants to finish school and go to college.

Yet she has a secret life...

She has spent years living two lives, one as Sam which the world sees most and one as Foresight, who Sam feels is her true self where she is a passionate and gifted hacker.

She has never found a system she could not bend to her will.

She is the essence of a true magician within the dark recesses of the web which many dare not enter.

Foresight and Sam never mix.

This is something that Sam goes to extreme lengths to ensure.

These two very different lives however may be veering towards an unstoppable collision course.

The weave of tension and intrigue grows beyond her comprehension as she dives beneath the deep dark corners of the hacker world to really discover what she is made of.